DEMON

At Clear Creek

DEMON
At Clear Creek

by Robert A. Powell

This is a work of fiction. All names, characters, places, and incidents are the product of the author's imagination, or are used fictitiously. Any resemblance to actual events or persons, living or dead, is purely coincidental.

Silverhawke Publications

Bayonet Point, Florida 34667

Copyright 2004 by Robert A. Powell

Manufactured in the United States of America

ISBN 0-9651406-8-7

This work of fiction is based on the legend of the strange activities believed to be caused by supernatural forces at work in Kentucky's Red River Gorge.

Prologue

Culver City was a placid, rural community, nestled in the foothills of the Appalachian Mountains.

The night was quiet and desperately dark. There was hardly a whisper of activity, especially in the alley behind Donovan's Hardware Store. Only the 60-watt incandescent bulb above the rear entrance offered illumination, and it was barely enough to distinguish the tattered sign, "Donovan's Hardware - Deliveries."

The large two-story building was an old structure, with no windows in the back. The door opened on to a 4 x 6 stoop, five steps above the parking lot.

When the small door slowly opened, a shimmer of light from inside solemnly spilled into the darkness.

James Donovan, handsome and debonair, was the 19-year-old son of the store owner. He came strutting out the door with two coworkers, Mark and Sharon.

James always closed the store on Thursdays.

Their jovial mood shattered the solitude of the night. James reached inside and flipped the switch to turn off the interior lights. The light immediately dimmed to a glimmer. The lone street light around the corner of the building gave Mark and Sharon very little guidance. They joked and laughed, as they walked down the steps and headed toward the corner.

James faced the door, searching for the right key. As Mark and Sharon turned the corner, they looked back at James and waved. He offered a sort-of half-wave gesture as he continued to fiddle with the keys.

His friends were now out of sight.

James watched the corner of the building for a few split seconds. In final desperation, he held the large ring of keys up to the single light bulb. He continued to fumble with the keys, quite unable to understand the problem.

He had done this many times, but the keys all looked the same. Exasperating frustration set in.

He tried two or three keys in the dead bolt. No luck at all. An uneasy feeling flushed over James. He sensed a presence. He stopped, hesitated, then quickly spun around, as if ready to confront someone on the stoop with him. No one was there.

His eyes frantically searched each distant corner of the darkness. He looked everywhere, everywhere, but saw nothing. Only the pitch black emptiness. Even though James was not satisfied, he returned nervously to the task of locking the door. The situation was now very serious. James periodically looked over his shoulder, as he continuously tried key after key.

James stopped again and stared searchingly into the night. Was there someone across the alley? He concentrated. Was it an obscure silhouette of a man? No, there was no one there.

He turned back. Besides, it looked more like a rather large serpent than a man; standing upright like a man; dressed like a man, except for that weird cloak.

He was definitely convincing himself, but of what? James shook his head. He was either hallucinating or going mad, stark raving mad. "Just find the damned key," he mumbled.

Success. Finally. The door was locked. James stood back. Satisfaction. He proudly turned to head down the steps, when a feeling of apprehension grasped him like a giant thunderbolt.

He stopped, mesmerized. His eyes locked on the serpent-like silhouette. James was terrified, frozen with fear. A speeding ball of light flashed through the pitch black night.

There was a brilliant, explosion-like flare on the stoop.

Total darkness settled back in.

Chapter 1

Sam Pent, a much-celebrated author, had moved back to his grandfather's isolated homeplace for the peace and quiet he so desperately needed while practicing his craft.

The cabin where he found that serene solitude was located approximately one-half mile up river from the point where Clear Creek emptied into Winding River.

On this particular day, Sam had been aware of commotion, somewhere downstream, within shouting distance of his house. He intentionally avoided the disturbance as long as possible, and finally wandered along the river's edge until he came upon the inconspicuous spot. A large crowd of people was gathered on the river bank at the mouth of Clear Creek.

There was some peculiar activity on the opposite side of the creek. Several Sheriff's Deputies and a few official looking people were milling around. They appeared to be searching for something. Some of the uniformed deputies picked up bones, scrutinized them intently and then carefully placed them back. Others simply observed with intense curiosity.

Sam quietly became a part of the assemblage on the east side of the creek. Everyone there was watching the strange activity taking place on the west side.

He surveyed the massive throngs, and suddenly spotted his neighbor, Carole. He gingerly made his way through the milling crowd, in her direction.

This isolated rural community fitly occupied a sparsely populated valley in the foothills of the Appalachian mountains. The divorcee, Carole Jackson, was Sam's only neighbor. She lived in the last house on the paved road, with two daughters.

Sam's cabin sat quietly back in a grove of trees, just beyond the end of the maintained road, down the hill, and around the bend past Carole.

The road originally extended on past Sam's house, along the river bank, to connect with Highway 10 near the mouth of Clear Creek. The section from Sam's cabin to Clear Creek was prone to flooding, any time there was a heavy rain, so the county determined it was simply not feasible to maintain the thoroughfare. After being abandoned for nearly seven years, it was no longer passable except on foot.

Even the culverts for Clear Creek and two smaller streams, which emptied into the river along the deserted stretch of road, had been removed, for use elsewhere in the county.

Sam slipped in behind Carole, and gently placed his hand on her shoulder. She was startled by the unexpected touch and immediately swung around to confront the intruder. She saw Sam and smiled. He didn't speak, but his expression eagerly asked for an explanation.

"They found some kind of grave on the other side of the creek." Carole pointed to the spot where some men were kneeling. Sam could faintly distinguish the men moving some sort of object around with their hands.

One of the deputies pointed to a pile of bones while talking to a couple of other people at the same time. The old bones appeared to be covered with dirty, leathery looking skin. Like old mummies of a sort.

"Some kind of grave?" He looked back at Carole. "What does that mean?"

"Well," she searched for a simple explanation, "it's not really a grave, as such. In fact, I don't think they know what it is, but there's lots of bones buried there." She leaned toward Sam, placing her lips very close to his ear and accentuated softly, "human bones."

"Human bones?" Sam strained to look.

"That's right," Carole continued, "those two little Jones boys over on Route 10 found them. They came down close to the water's edge to dig for fishing worms in the moist soil along the creek bank, and accidentally uncovered a skull. They ran home and told their mother. She called Sheriff McNeal, and that set the wheels in motion."

Sam was perplexed. "That is really weird."

Carole was alarmed. "Scary. You know I live alone with two impressionable young ladies … since my divorce. And, with all these bones …"

"Oh," Sam interjected quickly, "I don't think there's any reason for you to worry."

"Probably not." Matter-of-factly. "When the Sheriff saw there were lots of bones, he immediately called in specialists from the University. That's when all the clamor came about."

"Specialists? What kind of specialists?" Sam inquired.

"Hunh," Carole exclaimed, "I'm not real sure. No one is saying much at all, just yet. Rumors are flying rampant, but it has really been quite an unruly mess."

Sam looked around. "I didn't know there were this many people in the entire county."

A small girl pushed her way past Sam and took hold of her mother's hand. Savannah, Carole's overly exuberant ten-year-old daughter, looked up pensively and smiled. "Hi, Sam."

"Hello, Savannah. Did you come to find out what all the excitement is about?"

"Me and Jess were already here, while ago."

"Oh," surprised. "You were?"

"Yep. We went back home to get a snack." She stretched her neck to look around him. Sam turned to look as well. "I don't know what happened to Jess. She was right behind me."

"I don't see her anywhere," Sam added.

"We ran all the way back." She swelled with pride. "I'm a lot faster than her."

"You didn't even wait for your sister?"

His tease didn't shame her the least bit. "Nope." Savannah shrugged her delicate shoulders. "Besides, she knows the way."

Oblivious to their conversation, Carole looked at Savannah. She then looked around. Her eyes diligently searched the crowd, then flashed back to Savannah. "Where is your sister?"

Savannah puckered her lower lip cautiously over the upper and shrugged her shoulders once again.

New activity across the creek interrupted Carole's attention. A van had pulled up next to the pit, and men started loading bones into the vehicle.

Savannah looked at Sam and grinned. She had gotten by for the moment. Sam forced a disapproving smile.

Carole pointed toward the van. "Look, they're taking some of the bones away."

Sam instantly switched his attention to the activities across the creek. A panel truck jostled its way through the crowd and parked right next to the grave site. Some men retrieved a canopy from the truck and began to erect it over the bones.

They stretched yellow tape, marked CRIME SCENE - DO NOT CROSS around the posts, and set another ten or twelve posts in a large circle about ten feet beyond the original perimeter. Then they proceeded to stretch the crime scene tape around those posts as well.

"What the hell?!" Sam exclaimed. "They're marking it off as a crime scene."

Carole glanced over her shoulder at Sam. "Well, I sure wish someone would tell us what's going on?"

Sam observed and considered, "They should definitely seal the area off until some determination is made as to what might actually have been discovered here. . ."

This brought reaction from another nearby spectator. "I heard Larry Smith say those bones are of prehistoric Indians."

Utter shock flushed Sam's face. "Are you serious?"

"That's right. He said that is some sort of old Indian burial mound. One that has evidently already been disturbed."

Another bystander stepped up. "That sounds logical. You know prehistoric Native Americans lived in this area as early as 8000 B.C. And, of the two-hundred and twenty burial mounds discovered across the state, three major finds are located right here in Beckham County."

Larry Smith was considered to be the state's foremost authority on prehistoric people. He had studied each and every burial mound within the entire state.

"Larry Smith is the curator at the Historical Society," Carole noted proudly.

"Yes, I know who he is," Sam responded indignantly.

The fellow who made the original statement turned to face them directly. "They also made mention that those skeletons are thousands of years old."

The second fellow jumped in quickly, "Skeletons! They're not skeletons, they're actually mummies."

"Yeah," the first man retorted, "that's right, and Larry Smith says that mass grave is not neat and orderly, like most of the usual Indian mounds."

"I see, not a well-kept grave." Sam laughed. "I guess that just means there aren't enough prehistoric people left around here to maintain it properly."

An angry frown. "Indians, modern, as well as ancient, were very precise." A stinging quip, with a deliberate pause to keep the attention. "Especially when it came to their dead. They were very meticulous about the care and preservation of the dead."

Sam injected, "Just joking. But they will no doubt carbon date those bones, and run some other tests to be sure, even if they do appear to be ancient."

"Like Miss Susie?"

"What do you mean by that?"

"They carbon dated her."

"Yeah? So why did they carbon date Miss Susie? Whoever the heck she is."

Carole smiled. "That's the name they gave that old mummy they found in a cave up on Turkey Creek, in the north eastern part of the county."

Sam raised his eyebrows. "I certainly never heard anything about Miss Susie."

"Seriously? You never heard about Miss Susie?"

"Not until now."

"Wow, she made International news. I never met anyone who hadn't heard about Miss Susie."

"Well, it seems they found a well-preserved mummy that was more than two million years old."

"Two million years? You've gotta be kidding."

"It's true. She was considered an exceptional discovery. They knew Indians lived here thousands of years B.C. but Miss Susie dated back two million years."

"How the hell do they know her name?"

Carole laughed. "The skeleton was a very small female, but tests indicate she was a fully grown adult. Someone in the lab placed the toe-tag 'Miss Susie' on her just for identification purposes; the name stuck."

"It seems quite humorous to have a two-million-year-old mummy called Miss Susie."

"But appropriate. She was discovered over twenty years ago. There are hundreds of caves and shelters throughout the area that are full of bones, but Miss Susie is actually the only complete skeleton ever found."

"That seems very odd."

"No. Not so odd. They say animals have used those caves and shelters as their dens for centuries. The animals and the elements of weather probably destroyed most of any remains. Miss Susie just happened to be in the right place. Lots of people have searched since, believing there are likely others, but she's the only one ever found."

"Maybe not," an old timer rebuked, "wait till they get the test results on that stash there." He pointed.

Sam watched the deputies for a few moments. "But why are they marking it off as a crime scene?"

"That's the only way they have to keep people away. They don't want the site disturbed until the mystery is unraveled."

"Well, I certainly agree that it should be protected, but it doesn't sound like much of a mystery. Sounds to me like they already have all the answers."

"Truthfully? They don't even have a clue. Even though there were prehistoric people in this area, no one is certain at this point, why this stockpile of skeletons are heaped into one big hole like that. It's total speculation."

Jessica, Carole's cute, slender, vivacious, thirteen-year old daughter, came strolling up to join the group. She nonchalantly

14

whacked her sister on the top of her head. "You little twerp," she muffled to Savannah. She looked at Sam. "Hi Sam!" she replied sweetly.

"Hello, Jess." Sam looked down amicably to acknowledge the delightful intruder. "Where've you been?"

Jessica flashed an expression of disgust, gritted her teeth, and promptly whacked Savannah once again. "Been looking all over, for my dumb sister, who ran off and left me." She glared at Savannah, who simply rubbed her head and defiantly grinned from ear to ear.

Carole swatted at Jessica's hand. "You girls settle down."

"I saw Mr. Brewer," Jessica responded forthwith.

"You did?" Genuinely intrigued. "Where?"

She pointed into the crowd. "Over there, close to that fella in the bright red shirt."

"Did he speak to you?"

"Sure did. He told me that all those people in that grave were murdered."

Immediate attitude change. Carole placed her hand gently on Jessica's shoulder to comfort her. "Honey, he doesn't know what happened. He's just guessing."

"Oh, he knows!" Savannah jumped in adamantly. "He said that's what happens to little girls who run away. Some monster kills them and puts them in that big old hole over there." She pointed at once toward the grave site across the creek.

Jessica glared at Savannah. "How do you know, Twerp? You weren't even there?"

"Yes, I was. I heard him say it." Savannah's eyes were as big and round as saucers.

Carole was not quite sure what to say. Could she honestly say there was no monster? This was indeed an unusual, baffling mystery, and she most assuredly had no intention of scaring her daughters. After some quick thinking, "There's nothing to worry about, sweetheart," she responded, "you're just as safe now as you were yesterday. Mr. Brewer didn't think either of you should be wondering around in this crowd by yourself. And he is certainly right about that."

"Those are not little girl bones, anyway," Jessica snorted, "Mr. Smith said they're old Indian bones."

"Old Indian bones?" Savannah looked inquisitively from one person to the other. "They don't look like no Indian bones."

Sam quizzed. "What do Indian bones look like?"

She looked up with a frown. "Well, I don't know! But they don't look like Indians to me."

Sheriff McNeal made a loud noise and held his arms over his head to get everyone's attention. The crowd got quiet. "Listen up, people. You can all go on home. Nothing else is going to happen here. We're sending some of the bones to the University lab for tests."

He looked around and pointed toward the canopy. "There will be a deputy posted here, to see that the rest of these bones are not disturbed. You all go on home."

As the sheriff spoke, Sam studied the crowd. *"Deja vu,"* he imagined. He focused specifically on the people gathered at the grave. The multitudes on the opposite shore. The noises of the crowd became a subtle hum. The images were static, almost like an old photograph. Movement slowly returned. *"It's the same crowd,"* he thought. *"The very same people who were here ten years ago . . . when that eleven-year-old boy drowned."* He slowly panned the crowd from face to face. *"They're older,"* he concluded, *"but it's the exact same crowd, in the same location, similar but different circumstances. How ironic."*

"We're leaving, Sam." Jessica tugged at Sam's arm. "Are you coming?"

Sam was jolted back to the present. "What's that?"

He looked at Jessica, then turned to see that Carole and Savannah were already pushing their way through the mob.

"Sure. I'll walk with you, Jess." Sam took her outstretched hand, and they strolled off.

Sam glanced back across the creek, then down at Jessica. She looked up with her beautiful smile and skipped a step to keep up with him. Carole glanced over her shoulder to make sure they were following.

Chapter 2

Sheriff McNeal was sitting in his office, quietly perusing a folder of papers. He shuffled the papers briskly, looked up with obvious concern, then quickly shuffled again. He slowly picked up his papers with one hand, walked to the doorway of his office and leaned against the doorjamb.

He held the folder at arm's length, glanced at it briefly, and then dropped it to his side as he strolled across the room to an empty desk in the outer office. He flopped the folder on the desk and stared off into space. Everyone was aware, but no one gave him a second notice.

This was not an unusual routine. It was his typical way of dealing with frustrating situations. His staff was quite used to it.

The deputies threw sporadic glances his way but waited patiently. They knew quite well the point of confrontation was close at hand, and that it would be totally useless to ask any questions before the sheriff was ready to proceed.

Finally, he turned to face his audience.

"Hey, Jasper," he declared rather austerely.

Fully realizing the procedure was now underway, the deputy looked up from his work, and responded quite frankly. "Yeah, Sheriff. What is it?"

"You're a God fearing man, aren't you?"

"Yes, I like to think so." Jasper was baffled. "I do consider myself to be a God fearing Christian." He never knew what to expect when the sheriff began one of these little exercises, but without a doubt, this question clearly threw him for a loop. "Why do you ask, Sheriff? Have I done something . . ."

Sheriff McNeal was deep in thought. He didn't intentionally ignore Jasper's anxiety, nor did he mean to cut him off so abruptly, he was simply caught in his own train of thought and frequently had a tendency to ignore everything outside his own mind, especially when he asked a rhetorical question as part of his deliberation.

Jasper waited patiently for the sheriff to continue. Everyone else in the room stopped what they were doing to observe. They watched and waited. The room was filled with curiosity.

"Well, do you believe in the Holy Spirit?"

Dumbfounded. "Sure. I believe in the Holy Spirit."

"Then," he searched for the precise words, "do you also believe in the Unholy Spirit?"

Jasper reflected for a moment. "Yes. That would be Satan."

"Satan?" There was an obvious questioning pause. "I never thought of Satan as a spirit?"

"Of course. Satan is the supreme spirit of evil."

"Excuse me?" The sheriff glared longingly, as if he had heard the vague sound of a distant bell through a thick, murky haze. "What did you say!?"

"Evil," Jasper emphasized. "I said Satan is the supreme spirit of evil. Most folks don't like to use the word supreme in reference to the Devil, but the word supreme qualifies the highest rank of something. And Satan is certainly the highest ranking of all evil spirits."

The sheriff nodded. "I understand perfectly."

He understood, but he was evidently still caught deep in his own train of thought.

Jasper shrugged. "What's this all about?"

The sheriff gritted his teeth, and tightly squeezed his lips together. He sucked a generous volume of air into his lungs through his nostrils and then made a long and deliberate exhale the same way.

"The bones. It's about that stash of bones we found over on Clear Creek."

Jasper was really puzzled. "About the bones?" He frowned. A strong expression of concern crossed his face.

18

The sheriff continued, slowly and deliberately. "It seems that Jerome Parks has some wild theory that we are dealing with a powerful supernatural spirit. He actually called it *The Unholy Spirit,*' but didn't mention Satan specifically by name."

Jasper frowned again. "Exactly what did he say?"

Everyone in the room was quiet but attentive. The sheriff leaned back in his chair and pondered briefly. Everyone eagerly awaited his next words. Finally, "He came by late last night to drop off results from the lab."

"You have the lab results on the bones?" One of the on-looking deputies asked abruptly.

"That's right." The sheriff turned. "The lab has offered some very fascinating data from their studies of those bones."

"Hey," Jasper responded, "what about Jerome's theory?"

"Those old Indian bones?" Sadie interjected.

Everyone, even the sheriff, ignored Jasper.

The sheriff folded his hands behind his head, as he reclined in the chair. He looked seriously at Sadie before continuing. "Apparently they're not old Indian bones."

The sheriff paused and studied the expressions on each of the waiting faces. "Some very interesting, and I might add, very unusual information has been revealed. They are definitely not prehistoric, as we suspected. As a matter of fact, they're not old bones at all."

Shocked expressions filled the room.

Jasper was perturbed that the conversation had apparently swayed off course before his concern had been dealt with, but at the same time, was genuinely curious about these interesting lab results.

"The folks at the lab have positively identified three people . . . from the bones we sent them."

"Identified? You mean they actually have positive ID's?" Jasper stared in anticipation.

Sheriff McNeal sighed and nodded. "Bones, dental records, DNA and such. Yes, they're quite sure."

His eyes briskly skimmed over the dumbfounded group. "That's where Jerome's theory comes in."

19

"What's Jerome's theory?" Jasper queried. He was about to get his question answered after all, and he was delighted.

The sheriff stared eye to eye. He continued with emphasis, "We have discovered, quite by accident, the remains of three of our more recent mysteries."

Sadie couldn't control her excitement. "Recent! Who are they, Sheriff? Whose bones did we find?"

Jasper looked at Sadie irately. *"Damn,"* he thought, *"that interfering bitch is determined. She is not going to let the sheriff answer my question."* He scowled and burned silently.

Sheriff McNeal looked earnestly at the deputies. "One is the little Smith girl who disappeared two years ago. One is the widow Brown, who vanished more than fifteen years ago. The other is the Jefferies boy who drowned in the swimming hole at that same location on Clear Creek, almost exactly ten years to the very day, that his bones were discovered."

"Johnny Jefferies?"

"I know what you're thinking. We figured he had drowned. But remember, his body was never found. Until now."

Jasper simply couldn't take anymore. "Sir," Jasper insisted. "What does any of this have to do with Satan, the devil, or an unholy spirit?"

Sadie interrupted again, "And why did they tell us the bones were prehistoric people? I thought it was supposed to be some ancient Indian burial mound."

"Well, shit!" Jasper thought to himself. He glared at Sadie. *"I wish to hell she would let the sheriff answer at least one of my questions."*

"That's where Jerome's theory comes into play."

"About the unholy spirit?" Jasper quickly jumped in once more, determined to keep the sheriff on track.

"Correct-u-mundo. Jerome explained that spirits thrive on energy. Some people think that spirits *are* energy. Totally . . . pure energy, nothing else. Anyway, Jerome has given me his theory, as a scientist. I've been thinking about his hypothesis all night, and now I want your perspective . . . some input from a completely different viewpoint."

"Sure. Shoot." Everyone was genuinely excited.

"According to Jerome's theory, something literally sucked the life force out of those people."

"Sucked? Like slurp . . . sucked?"

"Yep. He thinks all their energy and natural moisture were siphoned instantaneously, with such a powerful force to leave the remains in that mummified condition."

"Mummified?"

"Dried. Calcified. You know . . . mummified. He said that's why the bones look so old."

"How?"

"Well, therein lies his Unholy Spirit theory."

"You mean that he thinks the Devil himself sucked the life out of all those people?" Jasper was stuck on one track.

So was Sadie. "Sucking out the life force definitely sounds pretty sci-fi to me. More like aliens."

Jasper was still curious, "How can a spirit literally suck the life out of anyone?"

"Okay, here's the deal. Jerome developed this supposition that some unholy spirit may have taken on human form. Or, is possibly possessing a human body. He thinks the spirit has to be revitalized periodically, with energy. Life force. That's how he explains that grave on Clear Creek, as well as the condition of the remains we found there."

"Wow, that's some wild theory" Rawlings concluded.

"Damn right," the Sheriff agreed.

"Couldn't it be some sort of alien life force that feeds on human energy?"

"Good God, Sadie." The sheriff stared in disbelief, then acknowledged, "I do have some serious concerns about some unholy spirit taking on human form, but I am definitely not buying into any alien theory." He shook his head.

They all knew there was more to come.

"And?"

"Well . . . whoever, or whatever it might be, there is quite obviously some evil coercion living among us."

"Living among us? That's a frightening thought."

They looked inquisitively at each other.

"It's quite obvious! Of the three skeletons they identified, one is fifteen years dead, one is ten years dead and the other is only two years dead."

The sheriff hesitated, and looked at the deputies, "Jerome calculates there could be remains of nearly one hundred people in that grave. And I would not be at all surprised to find some of our most recent missing persons cases there."

He let out a deep audible breath, though it was clearly not a sigh of relief. "And it's also quite possible there might be other such graves around."

Now, that was a frightening thought. The room was so still, you would have heard a pin drop.

"Perhaps his theory is simply not valid. Purely an imaginary fantasy," Rawlings offered.

Sheriff McNeal shrugged. "Well, even if it isn't true, we still have a very serious problem to deal with."

They all looked at each other again, and back at the sheriff. "How's that?"

"At the very least, it means we have a serial killer at work in our midst. Whether it's an evil spirit, an evil person," threw a glance at Sadie, "or even an evil alien, one thing is for certain, some damned evil force is causing these horrible crimes. A grave full of bones. Bones of people who were possibly victims of some serious crime that we never even investigated."

"A serial killer?"

"Serial killer . . . right here in Culver City."

"Quite definitely. And, we are not certain at this point just how long he's been at work in our tranquil community."

"Widow Brown vanished fifteen years ago."

"That only indicates that he has been at work for at least fifteen years. Remember, we have only identified three victims so far. There are many more, and some could go back much further than fifteen years. And, of course, some might even be more recent than two."

"How can we be sure that all those people were all killed by the same person?"

"I'm not sure of anything. Undoubtedly, at the present time, we don't know much at all."

"Then how can you even suggest that it's the work of a serial killer?"

"For one thing, while it's possible that grave was used by more than one person, it's not very likely. That fact alone does suggest a serial killer. However, you do have a point . . . there's no hard evidence of any sort, yet."

"Were they all killed the same way?"

"We don't even know they were killed. All we have are bones. And, unless there is obvious trauma, it's extremely difficult to determine an exact cause of death from bones. None of the bones examined thus far have any indication of violent death. No bullets, no sharp instruments, no blows from blunt objects, nothing. That's partly the reason Jerome came up with his speculation, that the life was veritably sucked out."

"Wait a minute . . . he thinks the life was sucked from those people while they were still alive?"

"Yes. According to Jerome's theory, that is exactly what happened. He believes the actual cause of death, was the life being literally sucked right out."

Sadie reiterated her concern. "Question Sheriff. Didn't the little Jefferies boy drown?"

"Yeah. How about that?"

"As I mentioned before, assumed he drowned. No body, no exact cause of death. That swimming hole was the last place he was seen. However, we dragged the river for hours and never did find a body. At this stage, we can't actually prove he did or did not drown. There's no indication either way."

"So, what are you really saying here?"

"It's quite simple. I'm just saying . . . that we have a lot of mysterious deaths to investigate."

"Investigate?"

"That's correct. We have to wait for the scientific data, but in the meantime, we should pull the files for all unsolved cases which include missing persons."

"How far back do we go, Sheriff?" Sadie inquired.

23

The sheriff looked at her for a moment. "I don't rightly know; guess we go as far back as we have files, Sadie."

"What do we investigate, if we don't even know a cause of death?" Jasper asked.

"It will be difficult, I have to admit. Especially since many of the victims were most likely treated only as missing persons. The files might not give us much information toward violent crime. We have to start somewhere. First let's compile a list, showing any sort of connection at all between the victims."

The sheriff stood, and started toward his office, then turned with an afterthought. "And, we need to focus on the area where the bones were found."

"Focus? In what way?"

"We need to see who has, or has had, convenient access to that area over on Clear Creek. Especially anyone with access over an extended period of time."

"What age person are we looking for?"

"We don't have a clue, yet."

"Wouldn't it have to be someone at least in his fifties," Sadie acknowledged. "The first victim we're aware of, happened fifteen years ago."

"Let's look at everyone," Sheriff McNeal replied. "We can weed out anyone who doesn't fit, after we have more to go on. The information is much too skimpy at this time to make any sort of limitations."

"What about the unholy spirit?" Jasper asked.

Sheriff McNeal pivoted around abruptly. "Well, Jasper, for the present time," he admonished, "Let's assume the killer is a walking, talking, human being. No spirit, no alien creature."

Jasper stared mutely at the sheriff, who totally ignored his unanswered curiosity.

The sheriff casually strolled into his office, sat behind his desk, leaned back and placed his hands behind his head with his fingers interlocked, and gazed quietly at the ceiling.

The deputies resumed their previous activities.

Chapter 3

A solitary figure casually ambled along the lonely isolated road just south of town. The ambiguous form was not distinctly identifiable, but from the initial crude appearance, seemed to be a male in his early thirties. His slim, masculine stature was adorned with tattered old work clothes, typical of this farming community.

A car headed in the same direction slowed perceptively as it approached the lanky pedestrian. He scarcely gave it a second notice. As the vehicle pulled along side him, the power window on the passenger side deliberately hummed to a fully open position.

The passenger reclined in his seat, and the driver leaned across to address the shabby looking stranger. He cleared his throat for attention. "Excuse me, sir."

The eccentric character cautiously stepped toward the car and peered at the two gents. They were dressed in casual attire, sporting clothes. Elegant, not at all cheap. "You fellows looking for the golf course?"

"No. We've already been there," the driver replied. "We're looking for some real excitement, now."

He smiled. "Well, friend, the golf course is quite likely the only excitement you're gonna find in these here parts."

"That's not what we heard." The two gents looked at each other, then back at the stranger.

"Oh?" He could tell they were quite obviously expecting a strikingly different reaction. "Must be some big secret I've missed," he declared, with some definite attitude.

"Well, I don't know how you coulda missed this one," the passenger commented. He flashed a devious grin at the driver.

The man now appeared to be somewhat agitated. "Perhaps if you'd be more specific, I could tell you if I know what it is you're talking about."

"Evil spirits, mass murders, and all that sort of thing," the driver expounded. "That's what we're talking about. Does that ring any bell with ya?"

"Heard it at the golf course," his friend added. "We didn't ask for any directions because we figured it would be easy to find something like that. However, we've been exploring on our own, for quite a bit, and can't find diddly shit."

The old man just stared at them.

"Well, does that mean anything to you, or not?"

He was trying to determine if he should just walk away, or spar further with these two quirky thrill seekers.

"Exactly what is it you want from me?"

"Shit fire, man," the driver declared, "we want you to show us where the damned evil spirit lurks. Take us to his favorite haunts. That's what we want." After astutely observing the man's expression, he added. "Of course, we'll gladly pay you for your services."

"How do you know I'm not this damned evil spirit you're looking for?"

The two men looked at each other, hesitated for a brief instant, then barrel laughed.

"Seriously," the passenger offered. He leaned toward the window. "We'll pay you a hundred dollars for your trouble."

"A hundred bucks, eh." This raised his eyebrows.

The unscrupulous character eyed his walking stick, tossed it into the ditch, opened the rear door and climbed into the car. The two men watch mutely, totally gratified.

"Sure. Why not," the old gent responded gruffly.

There was a cooler on the floor behind the driver's seat, and beer cans in both cup holders on the console between the two men.

"You fellows been drinking a little, I see."

"We played eighteen holes of golf today," the passenger explained with a half-laugh. "It just ain't American to play that many holes, without consuming a few beers." He leaned across the back of the seat and extended his open hand to the old gent, "My name's Fred."

Fred gripped the stranger's hand and gestured toward the driver. "That's Dick." The driver looked back and smiled. The stranger looked from one to the other and nodded. "Glad to meet you. Just call me Scratch."

The amenities were out of the way.

"So, Scratch" Dick inquired, "where to?"

"How much excitement do ya want?"

"As much as we can get. The thrill of the chase. The hunt. We want to pursue the Demon, experience the excitement of sitting in his lair." Fred was utterly enthusiastic.

Dick glanced over his shoulder, "We want to confront the old sombitch on his own turf."

"Whew-e-e, that sounds more like frivolous danger than excitement."

"Have a beer," Fred offered with a jovial attitude, as he held up a can. "Maybe some liquid courage will help you enjoy the adventure a little more."

"Sure, I'll take a beer." He extended his hand to accept the offer. "But I sure as hell don't believe it will turn this fiasco into any sort of enjoyable adventure."

Scratch leaned forward and pointed toward the road ahead. "Head straight down this road. Turn right at that four-way stop just ahead."

They drove approximately twelve miles east of Culver City on an old narrow, winding, two-lane mountain road. Scratch directed them to a graveled State Park road, which took them to a camping area some three miles off the paved road. They pulled into a deserted parking area and stopped.

"Is this it?" Sounding slightly disappointed.

"Take another drink of courage," Scratch offered. "Then we'll walk down that trail, deep into the lair of the Unholy Supernatural Spirit that dwells here in Beckham County."

"Cool."

The anxious adventurers looked at each other with excited anticipation. They finished off their drinks and got out of the car. Their faces expressed sheer consternation.

It was an awesome setting, located deep within the Daniel Boone National Forest. From the front of the car, one trail led off down a ravine to the river. Another continued along the ridge that the road had followed to this spot.

The sky was not visible because of the enormous trees. Although it was mid-afternoon, it seemed more like dusk, or perhaps early evening. The three men surveyed the entire scene quite extensively.

Their guide motioned for them to come to the spot where he was standing. The men cautiously made their way to him. Scratch pointed toward an opening through the trees.

"See that magnificent rock formation protruding above the mountain top there?"

He checked to make sure they were looking in the right direction, then back toward the mountain in the distance.

"The one that extends from the gorge floor into the sky, like a giant tower." Dick and Fred put their faces to his hand and took aim with his finger.

"Yeah," Fred responded, "I see it."

"So do I," Dick admonished.

"That," he declared, "is known as Satan's Peak."

The two men ogled each other in amazement, and then looked back at the tall rock formation.

"Can you feel it?" Scratch looked around. He inhaled a deep breath as he stretched backward. He gazed at the two novices and spoke with precise diction. "There is evil in the air."

The two outsiders looked at each other anxiously. They were very uneasy. They looked all around.

"Well?" he repeated his question. "Can you feel it? Can you feel his presence? A hunter must be able to sense his prey. We're on his turf now; in his domain. You must be constantly alert and ever perceptive."

The smell of fear grew intense.

If terror is a synonym for excitement, these two adventurers were rapidly approaching their goal. The suggestions had a tremendous impact. They were now clearly filled with fear, but still, they didn't panic.

They slowly checked the surrounding area as best they could, under these unique circumstances.

"His domain? You mean we're in his den?"

"Very close," Scratch acknowledged. "But I'm sure the old sombitch," he sneered indignantly, "considers this entire area to be part of his home. What you might actually call his den, is down that path a short piece." He pointed toward the trail leading to the river.

The men looked at each other.

"Do we dare?" Fred asked frantically.

"Whoa there. You've come this far," their iniquitous leader reminded them. "It seems a shame to be so close and not actually sit in his den."

"He's right," Dick agreed. "Excitement is what we wanted." He flopped the palm of his hand flat against his heart. "Let's do it, Fred." He looked right at Scratch. "Lead on, my friend."

That brought a smile to his lips, and Scratch led them down the path. He spotted a nice walking stick and left the trail to retrieve it. The two men watched, patiently. He picked the stick up and turned it end over end as he cleaned off the burrs and prickly twigs. He held it up. It met with his approval, and he returned to the waiting cohorts, to continue the trek.

"What's that for? Protection against the demon?"

Scratch laughed. "No. Merely a walking stick," he declared. "I always carry one, especially when I'm in the woods. Just an old habit, nothing more."

"Don't we need one?" Fred inquired.

"Need? No, it's not at all necessary. I always feel more comfortable with a walking stick."

Dick looked around. "I'd really like to have one if you see another."

"Sure. No problem."

They rounded the hill and came to a large open area. The mouth of a big cave was at one side of the clearing, facing the river, which was across the open space, at the bottom of a steep slope.

"Wow!" the men exclaimed. They walked to the brink of the enormous opening, looked up, then from side to side. The opening in the hillside was at least forty feet high and sixty to seventy feet across. They calmly strolled across the vacant area to the edge of the cliff, and looked at the river, far below, quietly ambling through the gorge.

"This is absolutely awesome," Dick declared. "It's nature at her very best."

Both men walked back to the cave entrance and stared into the blackness. Scratch held his position, as he curiously watched them survey the scene.

"How far does this cave go into the mountain?"

"All the way."

They turned and stared blankly.

"Yep, it goes completely through the mountain," Scratch explained, "but you can't stand upright all the way. There are some large caverns between here and the other side, but there are also several places where you have to crawl on your hands and knees to get through."

"Have you been all the way through?"

"Oh, yes. More than once, I must admit. However, it's not always passable." He pointed to a stream of water near the entrance. "That there crick runs through the cave, and it blocks passage sometimes, where the cave is shallow."

Alarm suddenly seized both men, at the very same instant. They turned to face the darkness, then looked quickly back at the old man.

"This is it," Fred shuddered. "We're actually standing in his den . . . I can positively feel it."

Their guide brandished a devious smile. "Yes, my friends, you are actually in the bona fide den of the Unholy Spirit."

"I didn't think it would be this easy," Dick remarked.

30

Both men looked around. "Where are the guards?" Dick questioned. His eyes searched furiously.

"Guards? What a curious question." Scratch was puzzled.

"Yeah. From what the golfers told us, I thought the area was marked off as a crime scene, with guards posted to keep people like us away."

"Oh-h-h, you must mean police guards." Scratch laughed. "I thought perhaps you were referring to some unholy gargoyle-type guards," he gestured with his hands, "to protect the evil spirit and his domain."

"No, definitely not to protect the demon."

"Ah, yes. The golfers were most likely telling you stories about that grave site over on Clear Creek, where all those bones were discovered."

The two confused fellows nodded agreement.

"You told me you wanted to see where the demon lived. You don't expect him to bury victims in his own den do you?"

The realization of the situation began to sink in, and the two daredevils were beginning to become very uncomfortable. Their bottled courage started to wane.

Their expressions melted. Scratch hesitated only so briefly, then wandered slowly away from them.

"There are no guards here, because no one even knows about the demon's lair. To my knowledge, no one has ever looked for his domain. Perhaps they're not as adventurous as you fellas." He looked back. "Or could be they've never even thought about it." Scratch flashed a devious smile.

The two men looked at each other. Now, for the first time, they were truly frightened.

"In fact," Scratch continued, "most of the imbeciles around here refuse to believe there is a supernatural spirit. The ones who do believe it, have absolutely no clue that the river," he looked down to the river at the bottom of the deep ravine, "which leads from this point, throughout Beckham County, is the real key to the Demon's domain."

"If no one knows . . . then how can we be sure this is his den? You could just be putting us on."

31

"Putting you on? Oh, heavens no."

"I hope not." Fred replied sternly, "you'll not get one red cent from us if this is some practical joke."

"Oh?" Scratch tilted his head. "It's definitely not a joke. First of all, there is truly a Demon living here in Beckham County. Secondly, no one knows about this place, because no one has ever looked for it."

He tipped his head back and raised his palms upward. "Can't you tell this place is filled with evil?"

"Evil? No," Dick stammered. "How can such a beautiful place as this be filled with evil?"

"Good question," his friend rejoined.

Scratch was clearly annoyed by that. "Evil is natural. This area exemplifies pure, unblemished nature. Maybe you were expecting some dreary old castle or a decrepit dungeon like in some horror movie. Do you think evil has to dwell in some disgusting and ugly place?"

"Well, yeah. That's more what I expected," Fred admitted. "Evil is definitely ugly. So, I envisioned some broken down, dilapidated old structure for his home."

"Maybe even a decrepit old graveyard?"

"That's right."

Dick chimed in, "Precisely. A dreary, mangy old unused cemetery, not a beautiful place like this." He looked around. "Even though it is sort of spooky here."

"Well, perhaps everyone else thinks the same way you fellas do. I suppose that's why evil can lurk about so easily . . . and completely undetected."

"Undetected? What about all the people that nasty old demon killed?"

"Now, that is truly unfair." His attitude softened a bit. "Killed is such a vicious word. You must realize that even an evil old demon must sustain himself, in order to survive."

"Sustain himself? He's killed hundreds of people!"

"An unfortunate necessity. Humans kill animals and plants in order to survive. The demon takes his energy from living things in much the same manner. It's simply a natural cycle.

People are probably the same to him as smaller animals are to you. Merely a natural part of the food chain."

"You don't think he veritably kills for the mere pleasure of being evil?"

"No, I don't. I truly believe that killing for pleasure is an evil created expressly by man. The evils of man stimulate the worst in nature, whatever is morally unacceptable, total chaos. It has nothing to do with survival, even though the evil spirit does thrive on the wickedness of man. The demon, as he has come to be known around here, draws life force from people for one solitary reason . . . in order to perpetuate his own existence."

"Draws life force? How does he do that?"

"Yeah," Fred echoed. "I'd like to know, too. How does he sap the energy from living things?"

Scratch stared at them for a moment and then looked around. They watched, trying to perceive what he might be looking for. He suddenly extended his arms into the air above his head. He rotated them vigorously in small circles and then pointed his right index finger toward the top of a tall tree.

As the two startled men watched in amazement, a large fox squirrel came floating through the air and landed gently at his feet. It was very much alive but apparently unable to move.

He aimed both index fingers at the small creature. He looked at the helpless animal, hesitated, then turned his back. The squirrel started to wiggle, then jumped to its feet and darted for the closest tree. The two men were dumbfounded. They looked at each other; Scratch was staring directly at them.

They were unquestionably paralyzed. They watched this phenomenal activity, but couldn't believe their eyes. The obvious big question, what was coming next? Their expressions quickly turned to desperation.

"You nearly had me acting like some despicable human," Scratch announced. He gazed calmly at the men. "Just to satisfy your stupid curiosity. Luckily, I caught myself. But all is not lost, you fellas want a demonstration, and I can use a little energy boost about now."

"No! No, sir. Just forget about the demonstration. We're satisfied. Take us back now," Fred pleaded desperately.

"Yes," Dick added, "that's actually much more than I ever wanted to know."

The two terrified men were squirming hopelessly, trying to move, run, escape.

Scratch strolled into the dark mouth of the cave, turned to face the men, and raised his arms. "Feel the excitement." He looked left and right. "There is no place like home!"

The two men looked at each other helplessly. They could move their heads but were totally paralyzed otherwise. Neither of them could move a muscle. Scratch gradually transformed into a serpent-like image before their eyes. Then, he walked around the two men, poking their energy points with his long pointy, finger-like appendages.

He threw his head back in a wild silent laugh. He stepped back, stooped slightly, and raised his hands from his knees to above his head, pulling out their energy; their total life force.

There was a brilliant flash. Streams of visible energy swirled powerfully upward. The whirling force instantly flashed to approximately fifteen feet above Scratch, then darted rapidly into both nostrils.

His entire body shook and quivered. He dropped to his knees, with his head bowed. He stood up and raised his head. He had transformed back to Sam Pent.

Sam walked over to the limp bodies on the ground, looked down and somberly shook his head.

Chapter 4

Jasper stopped at the door to the sheriff's office. He had a large rolled-up map tucked under his arm, and he fumbled awkwardly with a stack of papers.

Sheriff McNeal casually glanced up. He saw it was Jasper, and returned his attention to the pile of work on his desk.

"Sheriff!"

"Yes, Jasper," he looked up again. "What is it?"

"I have that information you wanted about people who have access to that grave over on Clear Creek."

"Good." Sheriff McNeal hastily pushed his paperwork aside. "Let's have a look."

Jasper sauntered across the room. He laid the stack of papers on the front corner of the desk, and carefully took the map from under his arm. He unrolled it across the desktop, looked it over carefully, and then turned it completely around, before smoothing it flat.

They examined the map together, painstakingly. Jasper shyly pointed with his extended index finger to the spot on the map representing the mouth of Clear Creek.

"Here is the burial site."

The sheriff carefully scrutinized the map.

Jasper meticulously slid his finger to Highway 10. "All this is part of the Curry farm. Josh, Henry, and Sarah have lived here since birth. They're all now well into their seventies."

He looked at the sheriff, then slowly trailed his index finger across the map in the other direction. "This land between Clear Creek and the Pent property belongs to the Bremen family."

He stood there looking at the map. He held that thought as if waiting for some great revelation.

Sheriff McNeal glanced at Jasper and back at the map. He was aware of the conspicuous lull in Jasper's presentation, and sensed some significant clue was missing.

"Didn't their house burn down?"

"Yep." Jasper nodded his head ever so slightly. "The entire family moved to North Carolina after the fire. None of them have lived in this county for more than fifty years. As far as I could find, not one of them has even been back for a visit in the past two decades." He looked at the sheriff.

Sheriff McNeal looked at Jasper, and waited.

"There hasn't been any human habitat on that particular piece of property since the Bremens moved away."

The sheriff leaned forward to peruse the map.

Jasper added, "It includes three hundred acres that runs along the river from Clear Creek, over to the Pent property line, and back up over the mountain."

"Hmmm. So then, you think we can rule out those people closest to the grave site."

"Yep." He looked at the Sheriff. "Sort of."

The sheriff concentrated on the map again. This time he didn't give Jasper a chance to continue. "How easy would it be to have inconspicuous access to the area . . . for someone who doesn't live there?"

"Somebody coming in from somewhere else?"

"That's right. Could someone, say from another county, for instance, slip into this area without being detected. If so, how easy would that be?"

Jasper raised his eyebrows and tightened his lips. "I guess it is possible, but certainly not easy." Jasper went back to the map with his index finger. He studied, then continued.

"Coming from town, you have to pass Pent's house and the Jackson lady's house, here. She has two children. That makes four people who would likely notice any stranger." He ran his finger along the road. "Also, they would come past these other four houses between the golf course and Jackson's."

36

"How 'bout, from the other direction?"

"Well," Jasper leaned over the map, and then slid his finger to the area. "The Curry house overlooks a large, open pasture between Highway 10 and Clear Creek. There is no clear access without going across their property, and there is no place to park a car along Highway 10."

The Sheriff stared at the map for a moment. A sudden revelation hit. "Did we simply overlook Pent, or am I missing something here?"

"No, sir. I was just getting to him, when you started asking those questions. Pent is the closest in this direction."

Sheriff McNeal traced his finger along the old river roadbed. "So, all this property between Pent and that stash of bones on Clear Creek is vacant?"

"That's right. Anyone could easily go from his house to the grave site without being noticed."

The Sheriff deliberated out loud. "Pent's house is not visible from the Jackson place either. He has perfect access. He lives there by himself. Not many visitors that I'm aware of. He is completely isolated, and it's an easy walk along the old roadbed to Clear Creek. Wow."

Jasper accentuated, "You can't drive it in a car, but it's easy to access otherwise."

"By car? You're thinking about carrying a body?"

"I feel certain those bodies were most likely transported to that grave from some other place." Jasper continued, "The Curry house does offer the same scenario; however, there are three old people living there, which complicates the situation."

"Actually, Sam Pent and the Curry trio are the only ones who have a totally private access to the Clear Creek area. Positively the only ones," the Sheriff concluded. "This is very interesting information, Jasper. Must be Pent. Damn, that was easy. Looks like Pent is our prime suspect. Now to prove it."

"There is something else we need to consider, Sheriff."

"Hit me quick, Jasper. I'm on a roll." The sheriff was so excited that he actually had a suspect, and he didn't want Jasper to spoil the moment.

Jasper continued cautiously, "Sarah Curry and her two brothers have had access to the area for more than seventy years. Sam Pent, on the other hand, has only lived in the area for the past ten."

"Hey, that's right; he's only been there ten years. Who lived there before him?"

"Nobody. It was an old fishing cabin."

"Fishing cabin? Whose?"

"It belonged to Sam's grandfather, Raymond Pent. He built it many years ago. Don't know exactly when. Their homeplace burned to the ground, and he moved his family into town."

"Burned? When was that?"

"Nearly fifty years ago."

"Hmmm." That caused a distinctly thought provoking, but inquisitive reaction. "Before or after the Bremen place burned?"

"Around the same time, actually. I don't have the exact dates, but from what information I was able to gather, both places burned about the same time."

"How strange. And both families moved away instead of rebuilding at the original site."

"Yep. That they did. One family moved completely out of the area, while the other one stayed within the community, but neither remained anywhere on the original property."

"That sounds very peculiar. Exactly where was the old Pent homeplace in relation to Sam's cabin?"

Jasper pinpointed a precise location on the map. "It was located in that hollow just above where Sam's cabin sits now. Before the paved road ends. After the fire, the Pents built that big house up on Main Street."

"So, where did the cabin come from?"

"I think it was already there, but I don't know for how long it had been there. Is that important?"

The sheriff frowned. "I don't suppose it really makes any difference. Mostly curious. But since the cabin was in the Pent family, Sam did have access to it all along."

"True, but no one ever saw him around here."

Another puzzle.

The Sheriff justified. "Actually no one ever had a reason to notice him. He could have easily slipped in and out of town, and no one would have paid any attention."

"That's true, but it seems to me that some people notice whenever any stranger is about."

"But, if it's someone who is not truly a stranger, you tend to forget the exact movement, unless there's a particular reason. Especially after a long time."

"Well, I guess that's right."

"Did the Pents use the old cabin after moving into town?"

"That old cabin was more for storage. It's where they kept fishing gear, boats and such. After they moved to town, the family and friends used it for weekend outings. Some people slept in the cabin, and others would sleep outside. It was quite a popular gathering place in the old days."

"As a matter of fact, I do recall people talking about the big fish fries held at the old Pent place."

"Yeah." Jasper nodded. "That was several years back. The old cabin had not been in use for maybe ten years when Sam moved here. He purchased it from his grandfather. It was in pretty bad condition, and Sam fixed it up. After his grandfather died, Sam remodeled it to live in."

"Instead of moving into the magnificent big family home on Main Street?"

"Never actually thought of it like that. He rents the house on Main Street to Dr. Stout and his wife." Jasper paused. "Like most folks, I just figured it was nice that Sam moved back and fixed up the old homeplace."

"There was quite the fanfare when he came back here to live, as I recollect. Big celebrity welcome. A famous writer like that, coming home."

"Yes, he was very famous. Everyone was very proud that he came back here to live."

The sheriff reflected. "You mentioned Sam's grandfather, how about his parents?"

"Don't know anything about his parents. As I remember, his dad left town right after high school, and never returned."

"That's odd." He deliberated. "Then Sam didn't actually grow up around here?"

"No. In fact, he didn't spend much time in this area at all, till he came here to live."

"Then, why did everyone welcome him home?"

"Because of his grandfather. Even though no one really knew Sam Pent, everyone knew his grandfather. Like a third generation cousin, who has never lived here, is considered to be from here, because of his ancestry. They're welcomed with open arms. And Sam did have several acquaintances here."

"Okay, let's move this along." The Sheriff shook his head vigorously in dismay. "Tell me about these other four houses. If they knew everyone's routine, any of them could sneak past Pent and Jackson undetected."

"That is possible. However, I really don't think there are any prospects here. These are all rental houses. They belong to Mike Patrick. The Patrick property runs along the river from the Pent line all the way to the bridge into town, including the golf course."

Jasper looked at the sheriff and ran his finger back to the starting point. "Above the road, it runs from the Pent property back over two mountains and all the way to the old cemetery across from the golf course. It covers several thousand acres. And none of the rental houses have been occupied by the same person for more than a few years at any time. The longest current resident has been just a little over two years."

Frustration. "Perhaps we should just let the information set, for the time being."

As Sheriff McNeal started to turn away, something caught his eye. "What's this red circle?"

"That," Jasper revealed proudly, as he peered at the map, "is the Circle of Domain."

Sheriff McNeal stood back. Confused. "What the hell is a circle of domain?"

Jasper concentrated. He wanted to present it properly. The sheriff had a habit of poking fun at his conjectures, and this was one endeavor, for which Jasper wanted proper respect.

"I took clues from Jerome's theory, and listed all of the unexplained deaths within a twenty-mile radius of that grave site over the past ten years."

"All unexplained deaths?"

"Well, to be more precise, I listed all deaths that occurred in that area in the past ten years for which the cause of death was not listed as old age, sickness or natural causes."

"Wow! Okay, I must ask. Why twenty miles? That goes beyond our jurisdiction in two directions."

"I don't think the serial killer gives a flying hoot about our jurisdiction."

"Maybe not, but I most certainly do. Now explain how you calculated your twenty-mile radius."

It was a crude response, but Jasper was extremely pleased. The sheriff was actually interested enough to ask him a serious question about his theory.

"Remember the Boy Scout Troop that vanished ten years ago, during a weekend outing?"

"Sure, I remember. That tells me why you picked ten years, but why twenty miles?"

"No, actually the ten years is because our records are easy to access for the past decade. It gave me a good starting point, and Jerome has identified some of the bones in that grave as belonging to members of that missing Scout Troop."

Jasper pointed to a red dot on the western edge of the circle. "This is where the Scouts were camped." He ran his finger northward. "This is the spot where they were last seen." He slid his finger to the center of the circle and looked up.

"And this is the spot where some of their bones were eventually discovered."

The line which connected the three points formed a perfect equilateral triangle. One point was in the exact center of the circle, the other two were each located precisely on the twenty mile radius.

"That's remarkable, Jasper." Sheriff McNeal moved his mouth as if performing some weird stretching exercises while thinking. "I'm not sure where we're going with this, but it's certainly more fascinating than my feeble hunch about the easy access." He ran his finger around the triangle.

Jasper beamed. He wasn't sure if the Sheriff was being facetious, but he decided to move forward. "I think you will find the rest of this information just as intriguing, Sheriff."

"The rest of it?" Sheriff McNeal leaned forward to see what Jasper was pointing out. "Go ahead, Jasper. You have my undivided attention."

"Each of these red dots indicates the scene of a mysterious tragedy that resulted in multiple deaths."

"Explain your use of the term multiple deaths."

"Any time there were a dozen or more victims who died in a single tragedy."

The sheriff frowned. "A dozen or more victims?"

"Yes. It all goes back to Jerome's theory," Jasper explained. "I've found that some sort of catastrophe has occurred within this circle each year between June and September. Every year over the past ten years, with the exception of one."

"How do strange catastrophes have anything to do with Jerome's theory?"

"He told you that some unholy spirit is sucking the energy out of people in order to revitalize itself."

"O-o-o-kay."

"And, that the evil spirit has to gain new energy in order to perpetuate itself."

"Right again, but I still don't quite make a connection." The sheriff settled back in his chair and flung his arm upward haphazardly as a sign to continue.

"Although I found one mysterious death each year that involves a dozen or more victims, there is also at least one mystery every four months which includes one or two people."

The sheriff scowled as he mentally calculated. "My God, Jasper. That's a helluva lot of unexplained deaths. I didn't have any idea we had that number of unsolved mysteries on our books over the past ten years."

"Well . . ." Jasper wavered slightly. He knew the next part of his confabulation was very iffy. "They're not all what you would

42

consider unsolved mysteries. In fact, we didn't even question most of them."

Now the sheriff was really confused. "So? If they're not unsolved mysteries, what are they?"

"Mysterious deaths. Big difference, Sheriff."

"What's the big difference? Are they mysterious deaths that are not actually unsolved? Or, mysterious deaths that are not really mysteries? I'm in the dark here, Jasper, but my main concern is why we didn't investigate these multiple deaths."

"Actually, it's the pattern that caught my attention. Not necessarily the event itself. The fact that a dozen or more people died in some incident . . . every year . . . within that circle, added to mysterious deaths every four months; that is what sparked my interest."

"Pattern schmattern . . . why the hell didn't we investigate these multiple deaths? Simple question."

Jaspers opened a folder from the stack of materials he had laid on the Sheriff's desk earlier. He pulled out a group of newspaper clippings.

"Okay, Sheriff. Maybe this will help explain."

He smoothed the first clipping out on the desk.

The headline read:

Multiple-car Pile Up on Highway 37 Kills 14.

A photo showed several mangled autos and the silhouette of a man in the lower right-hand corner observing the tragedy.

"There was that twenty-two car pile-up last June," Jasper explained, as he flipped the next clipping. And the apartment fire the year before." The headline read:

Apartment Fire in Culver City Takes 12 Lives.

The sheriff glared at him. "I see what you mean, Jasper. That is certainly no unsolved mystery."

Jasper ignored him and straightened out the next clipping.

The headline read: *Church Bus Tragedy Claims 13.*

The sheriff started squirming. Jasper hoped he would be able to finish before the sheriff's tolerance level peaked.

"The year before that, there was the accident with the church bus in July. While taking those kids on a field trip, it mysteriously ran into the river. Thirteen deaths, including the bus driver and two chaperons. Before that, the Reed fellow went berserk and killed those eleven people."

He placed the clipping on top. The headline read:

Reed Goes Berserk, Kills 11.

He quickly placed the next clipping on top, barely giving the Sheriff time to read the headline.

Disaster at Roller Rink Claims 17 Lives.

"Before that, there was the incident at the roller rink that caused seventeen deaths."

Jasper could see the anxiety building quickly in the sheriff's face, so he attempted to speed the pace.

"The outing in the park, where fourteen sorority girls from the college disappeared . . . the explosion at the power plant that killed fifteen workers . . . and finally, the Boy Scout Troop that vanished here, ten years ago."

Jasper looked at the Sheriff. "There has been some major tragedy every year within this twenty-mile radius. Every year."

The sheriff shook in disbelief. "I don't know what to say, Jasper. These are certainly tragedies, but not murders."

Jasper was very excited. "Exactly. That's why it's the perfect crime." He looked down at the map. Quite bewildered. "But I couldn't find anything for 1990."

"How about the alien abduction?" Sadie queried.

Jasper and Sheriff McNeal snapped around to discover the entire staff gathered at the door to hear Jasper's dissertation.

"Alien abduction?" the sheriff exclaimed. "Damn! This is getting too strange for comfort."

"I remember that," Deputy Rawlings added. "Twenty-two head of cattle vanished from old man Caldwell's place without a trace. Yep, that was in July of 1990."

"Life force!" Sadie added quickly. "Cattle provide the same life force of energy that humans do."

Jasper perused the map and pinpointed the Caldwell farm. He looked at his data sheets. "It fits the pattern all right."

"Pattern? There's that damn pattern again."

"That's right, Sheriff. We'd better be on guard."

"On guard? For what? What did I miss? Am I the only one missing the point, here?"

Deputy Rawlings spread the clippings out across the desk. "Hey, Sheriff, notice anything weird about these pictures?"

The entire staff gathered to peer at the photos.

Sadie grabbed one and exclaimed, "I certainly do. Look," she spread the pictures, "that man is in every photo."

She examined several clippings.

The Sheriff picked one up and held it toward the light. "I think you're plucking at straws here, Sadie. You can't even tell if it's a man or not. Just looks like a dark shadow."

Sadie admonished, "Silhouette. Quite distinguishable."

Jasper was not at all happy that his presentation had been interrupted. "Never mind that," he shouted, "this is June. The next tragedy is due this year in July. According to the pattern, it will take place right about here."

The sheriff looked at the map, then quickly stood to an upright position. He displayed an angry frown.

"For heaven sakes, Jasper. With everything from missing Boy Scouts and sorority girls to an apartment fire; even that car pile-up and roller skaters killed in a thunderstorm. How the hell do you expect us to be on guard?"

That was truly a viable question, and everyone turned to Jasper, anxiously awaiting the answer.

"I'm glad you asked, Sheriff." Jasper proudly placed his finger precisely on the map. "Do you know what's here?"

The sheriff looked closely at the map. "The golf course."

"There are two events that could provide enough victims for a mass tragedy at the golf course in July, but only one that is genuinely a logical selection for our next catastrophe."

"Logical selection? For God's sake, Jasper, please, tell me about your logical selection for a catastrophe."

Jasper ignored the sheriff's disgruntled attitude and calmly continued. "There are two major activities scheduled at the golf course in July that will bring in a lot of people. The Lions Club's July 4th fireworks display, and a big golf tournament set for the third weekend."

"You have put a lot of thought into this, Jasper."

"Yes sir, I have."

"Did you ever stop to consider the number of people who play golf there just about any hour, of any day?"

"No sir, I was looking for some special event."

"Why? It would be easy to kill at least a dozen people at the golf course almost any time you choose, without waiting."

"I guess you could say that."

"Then why will it occur around a special event?"

"Call it a hunch."

"All the other mishaps seemed to be spontaneous. Can you justify your hunch?"

Jasper was becoming flustered. "Let's look at some of the specific details of previous tragedies." Jasper flipped through his notes. "Take the Reed tragedy."

"Sure. Let's see if I can field that one. Follow your notes, Jasper, to keep an accurate check." The sheriff stretched back in the chair and stared at the ceiling. "As best I remember, Ariel Reed's sister was moving out of the county. The family and friends decided to throw her a farewell party. Ariel was not too thrilled that she was getting all the attention, but there were no indications of violence." He looked for confirmation.

"Correct."

"Even though he was very angry with her."

"Still correct."

"He was carving the roasted pig when she walked through the door. From what I could determine, all she did was speak to him. Bam! He went berserk. He sliced her throat before anyone could stop him. Then, when a couple of the brothers tried to subdue him, he killed them and randomly started taking the lives of others present. He killed eleven people, then himself."

Jasper just stood there, looking despondent. "Did I miss the point, Sheriff?"

"Miss the point? I think I've been missing the point all afternoon. But the point I'm trying to make here, Jasper; it was spontaneous! Not planned around any special event, like a fireworks show or golf tourney."

"It was a bon voyage party," Jasper attested. "A very big celebration by most standards."

The sheriff scowled. "Okay, you're right. Bad example. Let's try another one." After a slight pause, "How about the skating rink disaster?"

"Okay."

"Nothing special, just a normal night at the skating rink. Storm comes up, unexpectedly. Lightning strikes, roof caves in, and seventeen young people are killed. Simply an act of God."

"Whoa. I don't think God was the cause."

"How about, a cataclysm of nature?"

"Okay. I can accept that."

Sadie waved her hand frantically to get their attention.

"You have something to say, Sadie?"

"Yes, Sheriff. That was a big party for the high school. It was Junior Class Night. That's why the rink was so crowded."

The sheriff squinched his face. "Okay, then tell me about the alien abduction. I don't recall ever hearing anything about that one. What sort of special event was going on there? What were the cows celebrating?"

"Don't know of anything special. It was during the summer of 90," Jasper explained. "Clem Caldwell came into town to report that his herd had been rustled. We investigated, and couldn't find any signs of rustling. There had been twenty-two head of cattle in his east pasture. All we found was some strange sort of discoloration of the grass. Each area covered the approximate size of a cow, and there were exactly twenty-two spots. The story spread pretty fast, and everyone believed the cows were beamed aboard some alien spacecraft."

"So, the animals were abducted by aliens?"

"That's what everybody thought. They didn't know about this demon theory. Perhaps at the time he needed life force, there was no special gathering within this Circle of Domain."

"Yeah. Many disappearances around these parts over the years have been blamed on alien abductions. Only thing is," Sadie added, "we've had lots of people taken, but none ever came back. In most other cases the abductees are returned."

"What's going to happen if the bones in that grave are discovered to be some of the alien abductees?"

"Hmmm. Can't answer that one, Sheriff."

"Tell me, what was the most recent calamity, or unsolved mystery? Disappearance or death?"

"We had a disappearance, four months ago. Sally Kidwell vanished off the face of the earth."

"Vanished! My God, man! Sally didn't vanish. She ran away. Certainly no mystery there. We all know what happened to her."

"Assume. Just like we assumed the Jeffries boy drowned. Nobody knows for sure. Nobody ever heard from her."

"Hell fire, I reckon not. She didn't want anyone to know where she went."

"Even her dearest friends?"

"Especially her dearest friends. She knows that psychotic husband of hers would find out one way or another, if anyone . . . anyone at all, had the slightest clue to where she might be. If she told anyone, we would have a murder on our hands, not a mystery."

"Well, it fits the pattern. Another disappearance that will obviously not be investigated. Another perfect crime. Maybe the demon got her too."

"The unholy evil spirit? It seems to me that you're buying into Jerome's theory, whole hog."

"Unless you show me some better explanation."

"Well, Jasper, a lot of these so-called mysteries, in your scenario, will likely never be investigated."

"What if their bones are discovered in that mass grave over on Clear Creek?"

The sheriff looked up. He didn't know what to say. That was indeed a question worthy of consideration.

Chapter 5

Sam pushed the clubhouse door open and stuck his head inside. "Hey Mike, you ready to go eat?"

Mike looked up. "You bet. Give me two minutes."

Mike Patrick, nice looking, neat, about 35, owned the golf course, which was approximately two miles from Sam's house. About halfway to town. There was a snack bar in the clubhouse, but Mike and Sam went out together for lunch about three times a week.

Mike spent virtually every waking minute at the golf course and had made a habit of getting away for a few minutes each day for his lunch break.

Sam traveled quite often for book signings and personal appearances but was normally around at least three days each week. This had been a regular routine for the past few years.

Mike was standing behind the counter, writing on his steno pad. He was concentrating. Figuring on paper. After a few more notations, he looked at the pad, placed the pen neatly across it, tucked them both underneath the counter, and looked smugly at Sam.

"Okay. Let's go." He came swiftly from behind the counter and was out the door in a flash.

Benny's Place, a quaint country restaurant which featured home cooked meals and friendly service, was located on the river, approximately six miles from the golf course. The winding two-lane country road ran along the river from near Pent's place to the county seat . . . a distance of some ten miles in all.

A typical Mom & Pop diner, the restaurant was nearly always hustling and bustling at lunchtime. A nice crowd was on hand today, with plenty of chatter. Country music was playing softly on the juke box.

Mike and Sam moseyed into the restaurant, crossed the wide open room and headed directly for their regular table in the next room. Mike waved and smiled at everyone as he strolled through. Sam acknowledged them with a simple nod and smile.

Betty, an attractive-cute, yet considerably country, waitress, in her twenties, was dressed neatly, hair up, with a pencil stuck in it, and a friendly smile that would melt an iceberg.

By the time Mike and Sam had taken their seats, Betty had already placed a tall glass of tea in front of each. "Sweet, with lemon for Mike. Unsweetened, no lemon, for Sam."

She stood straight and reached behind her back to fiddle with her apron strings. She looked from one to the other. "So, how's it going, guys?"

Mike and Sam looked up. Menus closed.

"Wonderful," Mike beamed, "couldn't be better."

"Absolutely adequate," Sam remarked cheerfully.

Betty pulled the pencil from her hair. With pad and pencil cocked for action, she looked first at Mike.

"Lunch special, Mike?"

He nodded agreeably.

"How about you, Sam. Tenderloin sandwich, fries, cottage cheese and peach salad. Or, do you want to surprise me?"

Sam smiled. "No surprises today, Betty."

She turned and strutted toward the kitchen with a walk suitable for adult entertainment.

Mike and Sam watched only briefly, then surveyed the crowd. Several patrons had entered. Most of them greeted Mike and Sam when they came in, as they passed, or even some after they were seated.

Wayne Hurt, balding, with a beer-belly typical of the 36-year old couch potato, was dressed in a ragged, but clean tee shirt and jeans. When he entered the restaurant, he spotted Mike and Sam and made a beeline for their table. He pulled out a chair and planted himself squarely across from Mike.

"Some excitement down at your place, huh Mike?"

"There's always something."

Wayne looked at Sam. Sam looked at Mike, then back at Wayne. They both looked at Mike.

Finally. "Well, tell us about it."

Betty set the plates of food in front of Mike and Sam. "I heard it was another alien abduction," she replied rather curtly.

"Alien abduction?" Sam was startled, as well as amused. He looked at Mike. "At the golf course?"

"Don't be ridiculous," Mike sneered. "There was no alien abduction; last night or any other night."

"I heard tell it was some spooks from that old graveyard," Wayne added, with a big grin.

Sam looked from person to person. "Somebody tell me what happened."

"They found an abandoned car at the golf course this morning," Mike offered finally. "That's all."

"Abandoned car? That's it?"

Sam was absolutely astounded. "These conjectures are all about an abandoned car?"

"Yep. That's all. Happens all the time, but people around here are always looking for some excitement."

"Turn a mountain into a molehill . . ." Everyone laughed. Betty realized her mistake. "Or, is it the other way around?"

"Yes, Betty." Mike remarked almost sarcastically, "I think you meant to say they make a mountain out of a molehill."

Embarrassed. "I never get it straight, but I think everyone feels that if they talk about it often enough, something exciting will eventually happen."

"Come on, Mike . . . this one's for real." Wayne turned to Sam, "Two fellows from the city came to the golf course yesterday. They played eighteen holes and left. This morning their car was found abandoned at the far end of the parking lot. Nobody saw them come back to the golf course."

"Far end of the lot. Toward my house?"

"That's right."

"Does sound very strange, to say the least."

"And nobody knows what happened to the two men?" Betty stressed quite adamantly.

"Actually," Mike declared, "nobody knows that anything did happen to them."

"Bullshit," Wayne exclaimed. "You know it did. How about the Sullivan boys?"

"The Sullivan boys disappear?" Sam queried.

"No," Wayne added quickly. "They were visiting their friend Jerry Brown. You know, that kid who lives between the golf course and Carole Jackson. Anyway, they were headed home sometime around midnight, and they saw this intense glowing illumination." Wayne used hand gestures to illustrate a volcano eruption effect.

He looked at Mike, then back to Sam. "They say it lit up the whole sky."

Sam was indeed interested. "And they said this bright light was coming from the golf course?"

Wayne was extremely excited. "Yeah, A brilliant, fiery light, like nothing they'd ever seen. It scared them so bad they ran lickety split back to the Brown's, and called their parents to come pick them up."

"What about the light?"

"They described it as several swirls of light, arcing from the ground, high into the air and then flashing toward the parking lot. Only lasted a few minutes."

"No," Sam admonished sternly, "I'm talking about the source. What made the light?"

"They were too scared to check it out."

"Why were they afraid of a bright light?"

"They're kids. It was very dark, and it's scary enough to go past the old cemetery. You can imagine how frightened they were at seeing some bright light they couldn't explain."

"Kids are usually curious about things like that."

"They figured it was either some alien spaceship or some creature from the graveyard. Either way, their fear was much greater than their curiosity."

"Some creature from the graveyard?"

"That's what I think, too!" Wayne exclaimed.

Betty chimed in, "Yeah, everyone knows the old cemetery is haunted. That's the logical explanation."

Sam looked at Mike. "I didn't mean I thought it was any old creature. I was flabbergasted at the very concept."

"Everyone around here truly believes that old cemetery is haunted," Mike quipped.

"Nuts, most people believe all creepy old cemeteries are haunted," Sam scoffed. "But what does the bright light have to do with a haunted cemetery?"

Wayne glared at Mike and smirked, "He doesn't know about that old cemetery, does he?"

Mike shrugged.

Sam turned. He stared at each of them. "What doesn't he know? C'mon guys!"

"Well," Mike began, "you do know that teenagers use that old cemetery as an initiation. Their test for bravery. To prove you're not chicken, you simply have to walk past the old cemetery at midnight, that's all. Did you ever wonder why it's such a big challenge to simply walk past there at midnight?"

"I know why," Betty exclaimed abruptly. "Dick McKinney disappeared there at exactly midnight."

"That was thirty years ago," Sam replied sharply.

"That's correct," Mike admitted. "And it has been the main focus of supernatural phenomena since. Dick McKinney was a football hero. The first athlete with any promise to come from this area. Everyone had high expectations for a fabulous career. When he was named the captain of the football team, his initiation was to spend a half-hour at the old cemetery. The team members left him there, and drove off."

"So? What happened?"

"That's just it," Mike explained, "no one knows for sure what did happen. When the team returned to pick him up, they couldn't find him."

"Yeah," Wayne interjected, "they thought he was hiding, so they pretended to leave. A few of the guys stayed behind to watch for him from the shadows. When the others returned, there was still no sign of him. They obviously figured he had already gone home."

"Tell him about the light." Betty insisted.

"Right." Wayne continued as dramatically as he could, "On their way back to the cemetery to pick him up, a couple of the guys swore they saw a strange bright light coming from the direction of the old cemetery."

"That's it!" Mike inserted. "He was never seen again. Not a trace. The old cemetery became a major prank scene for the teens . . . and the number one mystery for the county. The bright light, as well as Dick McKinney's disappearance."

"I just can't believe one strange disappearance made it a haunted cemetery," Sam retorted.

"Many legends are based on less," Mike noted, "but there have actually been five more disappearances since that time."

Betty was surprised. "Wow, I didn't know that."

"Probably more than that," Wayne acknowledged. "It's five that we know about."

Betty quickly looked toward the kitchen, then turned to retreat. "I better get back to work, or I'll be the seventh to disappear." She rushed off.

Wayne stood, and pushed his chair under the table. "Yeah, I better join Larry and the guys in the other room. Catch you fellas later."

Mike and Sam were left alone. They returned quietly to their lunch. Both appeared deep in thought as they ate.

"I'm still interested," Sam acknowledged.

Mike looked at him. "Okay, what do you want to know?" he asked between bites.

"You know more than you're telling. I think you know the real connection between the bright light and the old graveyard."

"As far as I know, it's strictly the fact that neither can be explained. Connected by mystery."

"I don't follow."

"Well," Mike thought a moment, "the way I see it, no one knows what, or who, is causing people to disappear, or how they vanish, and there is absolutely no trace of any sort."

"Okay. That part I do understand."

"Well, no one can explain the bright light. There is nothing we know of that can cause such illumination."

"How about the golf course lights?"

"Nope. There's nothing at the golf course that can create any light like that."

"How does the alien abduction fit in?"

Mike laughed. "It doesn't fit in."

"Seriously. Someone obviously believes it."

"You know that all traditional stories about flying saucers and aliens embody creatures with exceptional powers. There is always a blinding light of some sort. Always a brilliant light."

"That's bizarre."

Mike put his fork down and stared directly at Sam.

Sam was uneasy. "What?" He asked defensively.

"You want to hear something really bizarre?"

A startled laugh. "Like all this isn't really bizarre?"

Mike looked all around to make sure no one was listening. "Perhaps something that adds validity to these absurd myths."

"Sure, let's have it."

"They're keeping it very hush-hush, but the sheriff told me," he looked around again. His excessive caution was beginning to give Sam the willies. "They found McKinney's bones in that grave at Clear Creek."

He took another bite and leaned back in his chair.

"Are you serious? Sam quizzed, "Dick McKinney, the first person to disappear at the old cemetery?"

"We-e-l-l-l-l," Mike conceded. "Yes and no."

"Whadda you mean by that."

Mike squinched his mouth and looked up. "He was not actually the first to vanish there, he was only the most famous."

"But, I thought you just said . . ."

Mike leaned close and interrupted. "I never said he was the first. My Dad told me stories about people who disappeared from the old cemetery during the last century. The legend of that old cemetery goes back long before Beckham County was even formed."

55

"You're kidding. Before the county was formed? I thought that old cemetery was created by the county."

"No," Mike grinned, "I'm not kidding. We built the golf course about fifteen years ago, but it covers part of the farm that has been in my family for generations. That old cemetery has been there for a very long time."

"Really? Whose cemetery is it?"

Mike leaned onto his elbows and stared straight into Sam's eyes. "It was started by four families who lived along the ridge more than two hundred years ago. Here's the real kicker." He paused for emphasis and looked around. "One of the families is my ancestors . . . and one is yours."

"You mean I have family buried there?"

"That's right. Every person buried in that cemetery comes from one of those four families."

"You know who's buried there?"

"Sure do. Your family members are all located in the back, northeast corner. I have all the information at home. I have researched and documented every cemetery in this county."

"Wow. I had no idea."

"There has not been any new graves in that old graveyard since long before we built the golf course. That's probably why you were not aware of your family being buried there."

"Now, that is fascinating. Very strange, but truly fascinating. Perhaps someone in my family is the haunting trouble maker."

Mike laughed. "Yours, or mine." He glanced at his watch. "We better get back, or they'll think I vanished."

"I'm ready."

They stood to leave. Sam picked up the check, but Mike grabbed it away. Sam reacted, "Hey, it's my turn."

"Nope. This one's on me."

"Okay then, I'll get the tip."

Chapter 6

Jeri Jacks spotted Sheriff McNeal seated at a corner table, with Mayor Bulan and Tom Simmons, one of the Beckham County Commissioners.

Bloom's Restaurant was a small town restaurant, classier than Benny's Place, and conveniently located in the center of Culver City. It was well past the lunch rush, and Jeri had been informed that Sheriff McNeal was here for a quiet meeting with Mayor Bulan.

Jeri Jacks was editor of the Culver City Beacon. The thirty-six-year-old, strikingly attractive female, was dressed elegantly, more like a big city working woman than a country reporter.

She worked as a news reporter for the Metro Daily for more than ten years, before she and her husband bought the Culver City Beacon three years ago.

Her return to Culver City caused mixed reaction among the citizens of this distinctly rural community. Most of them considered her to be a big city society girl. They felt she was using her position as editor of the newspaper to gain some sort of special notoriety for an, as yet undisclosed, agenda. Most of the people actually resented her.

The restaurant was nearly empty. A lone waitress was busy clearing tables. She looked up, saw Jeri standing in the foyer, and came nonchalantly, to greet her.

"Table for one, Ms. Jacks?"

"I'm looking for Sheriff McNeal."

Somewhat baffled, the waitress turned and looked toward McNeal. "He's right there," she pointed, "with Mayor Bulan and Commissioner Simmons."

Jeri looked. "Oh, yes. I'll wait here."

Blankly. "As you wish." The waitress returned to her chore of cleaning tables.

Jeri lingered in the lobby for a few minutes. Sure enough, Bulan and Simmons stood. They were leaving. The sheriff was still nursing his coffee. Jeri knew she had to time it just right. She gingerly nodded a pleasant greeting to Mayor Bulan and Commissioner Simmons as they approached.

"Hello Jeri," the Mayor greeted, jovially. "What big story are you working on today?"

Jeri didn't have time for amenities. "No breaking news at the moment, Mayor. Good to see you."

She was anxious to reach McNeal. Mayor Bulan was slightly embarrassed by the quick brush-off he received in front of the commissioner.

Jeri quickly made her way through the maze of tables in the most direct route she could maneuver.

"Good to see you, too!" the Mayor expressed with attitude . . . apparently to himself.

Jeri approached McNeal, who was reading a piece of paper. "Hello, Sheriff." She flashed a big smile.

Sheriff McNeal looked up casually. "Hello, Jeri. And how is Culver City's ace reporter, today?"

"I'm just great, Sheriff." She replied, without the slightest hesitation, "I have some information I want you to verify." She flipped her pad open.

Sheriff McNeal had no problems at all with Jeri. In fact, he thoroughly enjoyed the pampering she offered, no matter what her motivation might have been. However, he did sometimes find it difficult to take her seriously.

Jeri was well aware of the jokes being made at her expense, but she didn't let that sway her from her ultimate goal. She was not about to be defeated by the frivolous attitudes of these country yokels.

Even though she and her husband purchased the paper jointly, he was actually only an investor. It was her baby, and she was determined to turn it into an award winning paper.

"What sort of information?" the sheriff inquired.

"About the enigma at Clear Creek."

McNeal laughed. "Enigma ... that's a new twist."

Jeri ignored his attitude, she expected as much. "How's the investigation going?"

"You know I can't make any comment about an ongoing active investigation."

"So, it's still an ongoing investigation? That's the problem. I don't understand why it's not solved."

The sheriff shrugged. "Whether you understand or not, it's still an open case."

She squirmed. She definitely couldn't give up that easily, but she wasn't sure how to continue . . . then an idea hit.

"So, how about if I talk, and you let me know if my facts are accurate. Surely you don't want me to print a story this big with incorrect information."

"Could be the same thing. At this point, I really don't know what sort of information you could have that I might be willing or able to verify."

Jeri was actually shocked. "Does that mean you don't have any suspects?"

"For what? I'm not even certain we have a crime."

"Now, Sheriff . . . everyone knows there's a crime? You found a grave containing hundreds of bodies . . ."

The Sheriff immediately interrupted. "We don't have proof of any sort of foul play. Nothing indicates those bodies are victims of any crime. That much, I can actually confirm."

"You're joking! Just how do you suppose those bodies got there, and why?"

"Now that, my dear, calls for speculation. Truly a mystery. We do have a theory, in fact, we have more than one theory, but we don't have enough proof to support any of the theories. That's why it's still considered an open investigation."

Jeri shook her head in frustration.

The Sheriff added, "It definitely does suggest that a crime has been committed. Suggest being the keyword."

"Isn't the unmarked grave itself a crime?"

"Grave insinuates someone buried them. We don't have proof that anyone did bury them there."

"You're joking!"

"No. I'm very serious."

"How do you suppose they got there?"

"It doesn't matter how I think they got there. Whatever I *suppose* is total speculation . . . a theory . . . with no proof. That is why we are investigating. I simply cannot spell it out any clearer than that."

"Then, you don't think it's a serial killer?"

"First of all, there's no evidence that any murders were committed. I'm not sure where you're getting your information, but . . . be very careful what you print."

"No crime. No murder. No grave. But there is a pit full of bones representing hundreds of bodies. Tell me, Sheriff. Just what do you think is going on?"

"As I keep saying, I can make all sorts of suppositions, but without evidence, I can't act on any of them. And what I might think, is definitely not for publication."

"Nothing?"

"We have lots of speculation, but everything we have at this time is totally circumstantial."

"What about the skeletons? No clues there?"

"All those skeletons do at this point, is make it a mystery. A very unusual mystery."

They stared at each other for a moment.

Jeri decided to try another approach. "Okay. How about a hypothetical situation."

"Situation? Are you going to present a hypothesis, or are you asking that I offer one?"

"For the sake of argument, let's say you do suspect some sort of foul play. I want to present a scenario . . . to establish a basis for your criminal investigation."

"I'm not sure I quite follow."

"Well, take the people buried there. You suspect foul play of some kind, and are investigating people who might be involved in this foul play." She folded her hands and waited.

60

Sheriff McNeal suddenly realized Jeri was still standing. He immediately pulled out the closest chair.

"Pardon my rudeness." He extended his open hand toward the empty chair. "Please have a seat."

Jeri glanced at McNeal, then, "Thank you." She sat down and waited patiently for his response.

"In order to investigate . . . either a hypothetical or a real crime . . . we have to establish some sort of criteria."

"Criteria?" Puzzled. "What sort of criteria?"

"First, there has to be some means to determine what sort of foul play is at hand. Proper guidelines must be established to gauge your suspects. And, of course, their capability to commit the crime in question. That is very important."

"Okay, okay. I get your point. Forget about the hypothetical situation. I don't want to waste your valuable time with that hypothetical crap, anyway."

Jeri leaned forward, and in a dreadfully serious tone, "I have some extraordinary information to share."

This statement hit the Sheriff the wrong way and prompted an unexpected reaction. "Oh my God!" He clapped his hands to the sides of his head. "Just what I need, more extraordinary or strange information."

Jeri was taken back. She simply glared at him.

He realized the severity of his sarcasm. "Sorry, Jeri. I don't mean to be crass. But, honestly, I have literally received enough extraordinary information in the past three weeks to last me a lifetime . . . no, make that two lifetimes."

Jeri was not so much offended, as curious. "I take it by that comment, I'm not the only person with bizarre facts?"

The sheriff shook his head. "Not by a long shot."

"If you don't mind me asking, just what sort of strange information have you received?"

"Sorry, but I do mind. I really don't intend to delve into that at this time."

"Well, Sheriff, I'll make a deal with you."

"A deal?" Sheriff McNeal laughed. "What sort of deal?"

"To share information with exclusive rights."

"So, what are you proposing?"

"I'll share all my information with you. If it's at all helpful to your investigation, or even proves to be helpful later on . . . then you'll give me the exclusive rights to this story. That's all I ask. I want to help, but I want to write the story."

The Sheriff pondered for a moment. "And, you won't print anything until I say it's okay."

"Sure. That sounds fair."

"Well Missy, You've got yourself a deal. Besides, I don't know who else would want the story, anyway."

Jeri raised her eyebrows. "I have a strong feeling you'll be pressured to reveal the story before this is over. Just remember, you promised me an exclusive."

"Perhaps you're right. I hope not, but you can trust me. I'll keep my word."

"Okay, here goes. I heard you were looking at the people who live on the north side of Winding River, within a close proximity to that grave site."

Shocked. "Where did you hear that?"

"That doesn't matter," Jeri threw up one hand to deflect his comment, "the point is, I did a little digging, and some eerie stats started piling up on one person in particular."

The sheriff became more attentive. His curiosity was now genuinely aroused. Jasper's search had turned up zilch.

"And who might that be?"

"First, I do have a question."

"Shoot."

"I'm not quite sure how to ask this."

"Just ask, for heaven's sake. Open your mouth and let it flow. That's the best way I know."

She could tell he was getting slightly perturbed. "I need to know how familiar you are with occult jargon?"

"On second thought, maybe I was too quick. I think I felt better before your intentions became so clear."

"What do you mean by that? Are you sensitive about the question of supernatural activities?"

"No, is that the eerie part? There is all of a sudden a lot of emphasis around here on supernatural forces."

"Sheriff, I have an uncanny feeling that all your mysteries are going to be tied much tighter to the supernatural than you can possibly imagine."

"Somehow, I was afraid you were going to say something like that."

"Let's start with the master of darkness, the one considered to be the supreme evil spirit."

"Oh shit. The damned unholy spirit again. Have you been scheming with Jerome?"

"Jerome? Jerome Parks?"

"The very same."

"Frankly, I didn't know he was involved. Besides, I've never talked with him about any occult topic. Why do you think that?"

"Because that was the first question he asked. And to set the record straight, his only involvement is doing scientific research on the bones from Clear Creek."

"Really?"

"Really. Now, please continue with this valuable information you have for me."

"But you didn't answer my question."

"Sorry, what was your question, again?"

"Occult jargon. I want to know if you are familiar with the cognomens by which the master of evil is known?"

"Cognomens? You mean, like Satan?"

"That's precisely what I mean. Satan is obviously the best known, or most popular. Some other favorites include devil, demon, Lucifer, Old Gooseberry, Old Scratch, and serpent."

"Yes. Those names are all very familiar. So what?"

"Well, all of these are names used by the master of evil, himself. The one we most generally call Satan."

"So, how does the master of evil use those names?"

"The evil spirit, whether being called forth in some occult ritual or coming to live incarnate among us, is predestined to use his own name in some form. It's his pride. It's his destiny. It's fate. It's imperative. He must use a form of the name, even if it's disguised in some manner to hide his true identity."

"You're saying he has no choice?"

"Oh, he does have a choice. However, his choice is limited. Without the name, he is without the power. The name gives the significance to his status. Without the crown and robe a king is still a king, but without the name and title he is not."

"Then, wouldn't he naturally pick the name which would allow him the most power?"

Jeri concentrated. "What I'm trying to explain," she paused again. "There are many levels of demons or evil spirits." Another deliberate pause. "The names I just mentioned can only be used by the supreme evil spirit; not by any of the lesser evil powers."

"He qualifies, but he still has options?"

"So to speak. Say, for instance, an evil spirit comes to live among men, he has uncanny supernatural powers at his disposal, but he must abide by rigid ecclesiastical guidelines. He must use some form of the name given to him. That is his designation, his strength."

"So, I'll ask again. If the name is so important, why not use the most powerful name he can?"

"Because, while he does want his followers to recognize his power and prestige, he definitely wants to disguise himself from those who might thwart his mission should he be discovered here on earth . . . among mortal men."

Sheriff McNeal glances at his watch. "This is one fascinating lesson in occult practices, Jeri, but I really must be getting back to the office."

"Please," she reached out to take his arm. "You must be patient with me for a few more minutes. I had to make certain you understood the significance of the name because the information I have to offer you is connected very specifically to that particular factor."

"Okay, you made contact." He looked at his watch again. "I can only spare a few more minutes."

"Did you investigate Pent?"

"Here we go with the questions again. I thought you were going to provide me with information."

"Please, Sheriff."

He breathed a deep sigh. "Yes. We did background checks on everyone in the immediate area of Clear Creek."

"And?"

"Nothing. We didn't find anything suspicious."

"Well, perhaps my information will change that."

"Before you get too far along, I might point out that Sam Pent has only been here for ten years. We know the mysteries extend beyond that time period."

"I have some extraordinary intelligence concerning that fact as well. But first, let's talk about srpent."

"Did you say serpent?"

"Actually I said S - R - Pent. I left out the periods and ran the names together as one word."

"Ah, yes. Sam Pent, ser-pent. Sam Pent, ser-pent. They do sound slightly similar if you say them quickly."

"The ancient spelling of serpent is s-r-p-e-n-t, the first e was added in more modern spelling. The name Serpent can only be used by the devil himself."

"You're stretching it a bit here."

"S. R. Pent. Sam's full name is Samuel Raymond Pent. What better way to camouflage the name Serpent. He signs his name S R Pent. I looked carefully, he does not include periods after the initials, and he never uses the full names of either Samuel or Raymond."

"So, because of this, you think I should consider Sam Pent a suspect . . . suspect of what, exactly?"

"He's Satan . . . walking among us."

"Sam Pent is Satan?"

"The supreme power of all evil, Satan, if you so choose, considers himself to be the serpent. And, most religions of the world also label him as such. He is proud of that designation."

"Proud to be known as a serpent?"

"Most definitely. If you think about it, the serpent is used in some sort of symbolism for almost every occult ritual or supernatural activity. Always to signify the supreme, the best."

"Let me get this straight. According to this theory of yours, innocents and nonbelievers would only know him as Sam. While followers of wickedness and evil would recognize him as the ultimate force of evil?"

"Bingo. But it's not my theory, Sheriff. It's a fact."

"Fact?" The sheriff threw his hands into the air. "Whatever."

"Okay. Let me read something straight from the Bible. Revelations, verse 20. Then I saw an angel coming down from heaven, holding in his hand the key of the bottomless pit and a great chain. And he seized the dragon, the ancient serpent, who is the Devil and Satan . . ."

"Okay. In Revelations, the serpent is called devil. So what?"

"The Devil, Sheriff. He's called **THE** Devil, Satan himself. This is only one of many references that go all the way back to the very beginning . . . of Genesis and the Garden of Eden."

"Okay. What else can I say?"

"The rest of the verse I was reading, says that he was sealed for a thousand years, and then must be loosed on the world. You know how it goes from there after the serpent is turned loose on mankind."

"Yes, I'm familiar with Revelations. So, if Sam Pent is Satan, it's frightening perhaps, but I'm the Sheriff. As far as I know, it is not a crime to be Satan."

"You mentioned that Sam Pent has only lived here ten years. Did you find any background information on him before he came here?"

"No. But, as I recall, he's some famous author. Most of the information we have came from your newspaper. What sort of background information, specifically?"

"Evidently that was my mistake."

"How so?"

"I can't verify any of my own information. He was played up to be this famous celebrity returning home. Everything I have, came from my interviews with the celebrity himself, or from data he provided. I cannot find a single shred of information about him before the day he actually appeared in Culver City."

That raised the sheriff's eyebrows.

"How about all the books he wrote?"

"The books can be found in libraries, but they are all out-of-print, and the publishers aren't in business. Maybe that's within his power, if he is, in fact, the supreme evil spirit."

"You couldn't find anything?"

"Nothing . . . nada, zilch. In his interview, he told me he was divorced. I can't find any trace of the ex-wife. She simply does not exist."

"He had to grow up somewhere. There must be evidence of previous existence."

"If there is, I can't find it."

They sat quietly staring at each other.

"Brace yourself, Sheriff, there's more. When I came to all these dead ends, I decided to track his father."

"That's a good idea."

"No luck. All I can find is a name, Ralph Edward Pent. But, do the same thing I did with Sam. Break it down to initials, R. E. Pent, then drop the periods and run it together and you have REPENT. What does it mean, literally?"

The sheriff waited patiently.

"Repent means to turn away from sin."

Sheriff McNeal frowned. "Now, wait a minute. The son is *serpent*, the father is *repent*. Isn't that bass-ackwards?"

"Only if you start with Sam. His grandfather was Shawn Raymond Pent. Everyone called him Ray. So he was SRPENT and his son was REPENT. I traced them back six generations. It staggers like that for each one."

"Whoa. Let me get this straight. If you go by initials, every other generation is SRPENT, and the others are all REPENT?"

"Hold on, there's another grabber."

"My God!" the Sheriff quickly interjected, "I'm not sure my feeble mind can take any more grabbers."

Jeri continued without hesitation. "There is not one teensy bit of information on any of the REPENTs, the only information I could find at all is for the SRPENTs." She looked at the Sheriff with an obvious expression of satisfaction. "Mind boggling, eh?"

"Let me get this straight. You didn't find anything about the REPENTs, but you did for all the SRPENTs."

"Sort of."

"Sort of? Did you, or didn't you?"

"Yes, there's some information on each SRPENT. However, no childhood statistics on any of the Pents."

"No school records? No medical records?"

"Nothing! No records or information about any of the Pents, before they were adults."

"Talk about weird."

"It gets even better."

"Better? You call that good?"

"Well, not in that sense, but it's very intriguing. Sam came here ten years ago when his grandfather became seriously ill."

"Yes, I already mentioned that."

"I checked thoroughly . . . I can't find one single person, not even one, who ever saw the two of them together, at the same time. Even for an instant."

"Wow! How did you think to check that."

"I don't know," she shrugged, "just a hunch."

"Hunch?"

"That's right."

"Well tell me, little Miss Hunch. Are you, in fact, insinuating that there is actually only one Pent, who perpetually becomes his own grandson?"

"Ahh-ha! You are paying attention."

"Is that reincarnation?"

"In a weird sort of way. It's only reincarnation if he dies and comes back as another life."

"So what is it, exactly?"

"Incarnation. In all ancient civilizations, the serpent was actually considered to be the incarnation of Evil. However, the Egyptians went a step farther. The ring as we know it today came from their Ouroboros which was the serpent feeding on his own tail. It made a circle and was the symbol of perpetual life. The self-renewal of nature. Down through time, it became a gold ring to signify everlasting. Never ending."

"Then, what is the significance of the REPENTs?"

"That genuinely has me puzzled. I don't actually have a clue. Perhaps someone who is more knowledgeable about supernatural phenomena can enlighten us on that matter."

"And just who would you suggest?"

"I don't know anyone. Your friend Jerome Parks probably knows someone at the University. They do have a Department of Parapsychology."

"I must say, you're an excellent researcher. I'm impressed. Do you feel confident that there is no more information to be found on Sam Pent?"

"To my satisfaction. I have exhaustively checked all the normal channels and even a few backdoors . . . thoroughly enough to make it a real challenge for you to pursue."

"You're right about that. This tranquil community of ours has suddenly become a horror story. I suppose the strangest thing, is the fact that even though we have swung from one extreme on the spectrum to the exact opposite end, there were no new tragedies uncovered. This has happened by merely reinventing situations which have already happened."

"Then how can it be suddenly a horror story?"

"Are you kidding? You, Jerome and even Jasper are telling me that we have some supernatural spirit sucking the life out of our citizens, and you ask me how it can be a horror story?"

"No, Sheriff. I'm asking how you can say it is all of a sudden. Evidently, this bizarre creature has been at work for many years. It has been a horror story for many years. No one was aware of it, so nothing was done to stop it, but it has long been a horror."

"I see your point. If you're right, a lot of the deaths, as well as missing persons we didn't investigate as mysterious deaths, might actually be homicides."

"You asked what crime has been committed . . . is death by supernatural power considered murder?"

"Legally, homicide occurs when one person kills another. No limitations on method. And even if he's posing as a human, I see him as guilty of murder."

"So . . . what are you going to do now?"

"That, my dear, will take some thought. But first, I will have to wait until I receive all the scientific data on the bones from that grave. Hopefully, that will give me some sort of guidelines."

"How long do you expect that to take?"

"I'm not sure, but the information we have received thus far came a lot quicker than I ever expected."

Jeri stood, closed her pad, pushed the chair under the table. "Please, keep me informed."

"Since you're not going to publish any of this until we have the complete story, do you think I could have a copy of all the notes you have at this point?"

She looked at the sheriff. "Sure thing. I'll make a complete set and drop them off." She started to leave, then stopped. "Sheriff."

"Yes, Jeri."

"Do you think I might be included if you do meet with someone about the supernatural questions?"

"Yes. I think so. I'll let you know." Sheriff McNeal smiled and added. "Thanks for sharing. It's been quite interesting."

That pleased Jeri. She headed toward the door.

Chapter 7

The bathroom mirror was cloaked with a mild layer of mist. Sam had enjoyed a long, soothing shower, that left the room filled with a hot, torrid fog; like a steam room.

Even though the room was quite adequate for both a dressing room and bath, Sam lived alone and made full use of the house for virtually every activity.

Water caused his eyes to burn. Not with soap or shampoo, just plain ole water in his eyes was extremely uncomfortable. Therefore, he always kept his eyes tightly closed until he was thoroughly dry.

Sam turned off the water, squinched his eyelids closed tight, opened the shower door, grabbed a towel, and briskly blotted his entire body. He dried his feet completely, and then stepped into his slippers, as he wrapped the towel securely around his face and head.

With both hands placed on top of his noggin, Sam fluffed vigorously, as he strolled nonchalantly into the adjoining room. He stopped briefly at the faint sound of muffled voices. He listened but heard nothing more, so he continued the drying process. Sam patted his eyes firmly to ease that burning sensation. When he heard the whispering sounds again, Sam instantly jerked the towel off his head.

He was standing there, stark naked, facing two young girls.

"Hi, Sam," Jessica greeted cheerfully.

"Jessica!" he exclaimed in anguish. "What are you doing here?" Total shock overwhelmed him.

Sam immediately realized his state of alarm and tried not to appear overly emotional. He didn't want to lay a guilt trip on his young friend. He calmly extended the towel, slid it carefully down his torso, and pulled it snugly around his waist.

Jessica patiently watched the awkward dance. "This is my friend, Jenny." She took hold of the other girl's arm and pulled her forward.

Sam noticed the young lass was eyeing his towel. He unconsciously glanced down to see if there was something awry. Nothing out of order, at least nothing was exposed. Just the normal protrusion. Perhaps the lump was more fascinating because of the fresh image in her mind of what it actually was.

This made the situation even more awkward. Sam adjusted his sarong and strolled across to the dresser. Jenny's eyes were even wider than before, intently watching his every move.

Sam looked at Jenny, who was keeping a keen eye on his towel. Her persistence amazed him. He knew that little boys were fascinated by a sneak peek at things forbidden. Now, he was experiencing the conspicuous intoxication from this young teenage girl's glimpse of something that should be as natural as daylight itself.

He was definitely not very calm about this. He felt like a nervous young man in some gauche sexual circumstance that would happen during puberty; like standing in front of the class while trying to hide a boner.

"I brought Jenny here, so she can see for herself that you're a real man," Jessica blurted.

Whoa. Things were definitely not getting any better. This thirteen-year-old neighbor brought her friend to see that Sam was a real man.

That dire statement brought utter shock to Sam's already fragile demeanor. He tried desperately to keep his composure. He pulled shorts and tee shirt from the drawer, leaned against the dresser, and stared at Jess.

"Why on earth would you want to show Jenny a real man? You should be showing her real boys . . . boys her own age."

Jessica flopped on the bed with a belly laugh. She was obviously the only person in the room who kept her cool, and she was unquestionably quite composed.

"That's not what I mean, you silly goose!" She slapped her legs, then began to take on a more serious aura.

Sam headed into the bathroom. He closed the door, and the girls curiously scanned his bedroom to observe the vast amount of intriguing paraphernalia scattered about.

Sam presently emerged from the bathroom, wearing tee shirt and trousers, and carrying a pair of socks. He sat on the bed beside Jessica.

"Then, what did you mean?" He began to put on his socks and shoes as he listened.

"Jenny's mother thinks you're some kinda monster. Jenny was telling everyone at school, so I decided to bring her here to set things straight."

Sam looked her in the eye, "A monster? Me?"

"Yeah, like I said, Jenny was telling everyone at school. That's why I decided to straighten her out."

"No disrespect, Jess, but most people would agree with her mother if they saw this old man standing naked in front of two thirteen-year-old girls."

Jessica laughed again. Jenny was still mesmerized. "No, old man. That's not the kind of monster I'm talking about. I mean a *real* monster, some horrible creature, like you would see in some scary movie."

"Just the same," he added, "it would be best if you girls didn't come bouncing into my bedroom without any notice, especially when I'm not dressed."

"Oh, that's okay. Nobody will know." She glanced at Jenny for a brief moment and continued. "Besides, I think that was probably the biggest thrill of her life."

Jessica leaned closer to Sam, "I don't think she'd ever seen a naked man before."

"I'm sure you have a valid point, young lady. I don't believe everyone your age is as experienced as you."

Jessica is obviously offended by his inference.

"Don't be obnoxious. I'll bet she's the only girl in our school who hasn't seen a naked male body."

"Are you so sure she hasn't?"

"Ha! Let me tell you, when you stepped out of the shower . . . man, I thought she was going to have a cow. I knew right then she was getting her first good look at mankind."

Jessica hesitated, tilted her head and raised her eyebrows. "And boy, did she ever get a good look."

Sam was not quite sure how to respond. This was not a conversation he wanted to have with a thirteen year old.

"Do you have any idea how much trouble I could get in because of something like this?"

"Not to worry. You won't get in trouble. No one even knows we're here. Besides, we just want to talk."

"Talk? About what?"

"We didn't come here for sex education. Like I said, I just wanted her to get to know the real you, so she'll quit telling everyone that you're a monster. We can talk about anything. . . anything interesting. About you. Some of your adventures, your books. Anything that will help dissuade the idea that you turn into some demon that goes around killing people."

"Where did all this monster talk come from?"

Jessica's attitude became more baroque. "Everyone thinks there's a monster running around the county, killing people. Eating them alive, by most counts. They think that's where all those bones came from over on Clear Creek. Surely you've heard all the rumors and chit-chat by now."

"Yes, I do know that. But I didn't realize I was that monster. Who fingered me?"

Jessica casually leaned back on her elbows. "What do I know? These adults are total ignoramuses! Probably because you enjoy living here alone, like a hermit. That isn't natural to most people, others are jealous of it. And since you don't take no shit off nobody, many people just want retribution."

"Retribution? I haven't done anything to anyone around here. Why would they want revenge?"

"Like I said, jealousy. Don't expect me to explain their fool perceptions. I'm just an impressionable young girl."

"It's bad enough to make me a monster. Why in the world do they think I eat people?"

Sam stared at Jenny, who was staring back. He repeated with a twist. "Do you really think I eat people?'

Jenny didn't respond. Jessica grabbed her arm. "Jenny," she was exhilarated, "you have to tell Sam your monster story."

Jenny sat beside Sam on the edge of the bed and looked at him rather shyly.

"There's not much to tell."

Jessica scowled. Sam was patient.

"Tell me anyway," Sam insisted.

"Well," she began, slowly, "I heard Mom and her friends talking about a devil monster that was eating people. They said everyone who disappeared from this area of the country was probably eaten by the monster."

Sam turned to look at Jessica, who immediately reached around Sam to grab Jenny's arm.

"Go ahead, Jen. Tell him everything."

Jenny looked down timidly and slowly raised her eyes to Sam. "They said he probably ate people from other places as well, and then brought their bones here."

"Why do they think that?"

She shrugged. "That's what Deputy Jasper told 'em. He said there are too many bones in that grave at Clear Creek to just be from Beckham County alone."

Jenny looked at Sam. Her expression was that of someone confessing to a serious crime. "Deputy Jasper says there are more graves like that in these woods behind your house."

Sam was flabbergasted. "More graves? They found more graves ... in the woods behind my house?"

"No, not yet. But, he says there are more."

Jessica was getting frustrated. "That's not what I'm talking about. Tell Sam what they said about him."

Sam looked inquisitively at Jessica, then Jenny.

Jenny looked sheepishly at Jessica, then continued. "They were discussing what sort of monster could be doing all this, and that lady from the newspaper said it was you." She hung her head slightly with her eyes glued on Sam. "She called you the Demon of Clear Creek."

Sam was utterly shocked. Jessica had a wild *'how about them apples'* expression as she watched Sam.

"That lady from the newspaper actually said that I was a demon? Just like that?"

"Well, what she actually said was that the monster haunting this county was the Devil himself." She paused and looked at Jessica, then back at Sam. "Then, she said that Sam Pent is actually Satan himself."

"Incognito!" Jessica threw in promptly.

"Yeah," Jenny agreed, "disguised as a man. That's why she called you the Demon of Clear Creek. She also said that you ate people just for the fun of it."

"Good lord . . . She's going around telling people that I'm the devil . . . in disguise?"

"Yep. That's what she says."

Jessica was extremely excited. She could hardly contain herself, but she was hanging on every word.

"If they think a monster is eating people, why don't they think it's a werewolf or some such nonsense? I never heard of the devil eating anyone."

"Me neither," Jenny admitted, "but I think it's because the bones were buried."

Confused. "Because the bones were buried?" Sam was totally dumbfounded. "Like the Devil even cares if the bodies were buried or not."

"Yeah," Jessica added, "they said burying them indicates higher intelligence. Get that. At least they realize the Devil is smarter than them. Higher intelligence."

"One of the men at the University said that even if bodies were buried just to hide the crime, a wild animal like a werewolf, wouldn't do that. He wouldn't care."

"I see. I suppose that sounds logical . . . if any of this nonsense can sound logical."

"Another thing, those are complete skeletons. They said a wild animal, of any sort, would rip his prey into shreds. These skeletons are neat and clean."

"Well, at least they think I'm a tidy monster."

Both girls laughed heartily.

There was a slight lull. Sam was digesting all this unusual information. The girls were simply enjoying the moment.

Suddenly, Jessica turned to Sam with a much more serious refrain. Her stare got Sam's attention.

"See. That's why I brought her to meet you. I wanted her to see for herself that you are not an old monster in disguise. Just a messy human in the flesh."

The girls both laughed again. Jenny was obviously more at ease . . . pleased that she confided her story. Sam's demeanor had lightened quite a bit.

"Thanks for the picturesque description, friend."

"I just didn't realize that she was going to be able to tell that you're a man, with one simple look."

There was another chuckle.

"That must've been the whispering I heard when I came out of the shower?"

"No," Jessica exclaimed excitedly and bounced to her feet. "Jenny simply went bananas over your trunk." She pointed to the beautiful hand-carved chest sitting at the foot of the bed.

Sam stood and looked at the chest. "Oh, yes. It's very nice. And very sentimental, as well."

"Sentimental?"

"That's right, it's been in my family for many generations. It has carried the family treasures around the world."

"Wow."

"The dragon design is what really set her off."

"Not just on the trunk," Jenny remarked quickly as she twirled around. She extended her index finger and circled the entire room. "There are dragons everywhere."

"Serpents."

"Pardon me?" She froze and frowned quizzically.

Sam looked at Jenny and spoke deliberately. "They are not all dragons. They are serpents. The carvings represent serpents in many different forms. From many lands, and many different civilizations. The dragon is the most ancient of all serpents, but it is merely one configuration."

77

"Well, anyway, I love dragons. I mean, any kind of dragon, and these are awesome. This is absolutely the most fantastic collection I have ever seen."

"I was born in the year of the Dragon," Sam responded. "According to the Chinese calendar."

Jenny's mouth dropped open.

"Me too!" Jessica exclaimed.

"Yes." She flipped her finger back and forth. "We were born in the same year, remember."

"That's right! You're a dragon, too."

"Do you think that's the reason I love dragons so much?"

"Could be." Sam shrugged.

Jessica quickly browsed the room, then tugged at Sam's arm. "Tell us about the dragons, Sam."

"Sure. Look around. Pick some out, and I'll share what information I know."

The girls quickly canvassed the room looking for their favorites. Sam also intended to pick out a couple of his choice possessions. Before he stood up, Jessica was in his face. She held up a large gold jewelry box. Jenny was at her side.

"Okay. Tell us about these carvings." She handed him the gold box.

Sam glanced at the box, then at Jessica. "I thought you wanted to hear about the dragons."

"We do, but tell us about this."

"This is Egyptian artwork." He looked at the girls, and then back at the box. "Egyptians represented their cosmological and moral ideas with symbols, most of which had strong erotic overtones. That's why it's easy to find an erect protrusion in many of their art pieces."

"Do you like erotic art?" Jessica was half teasing.

He shrugged. "Not especially. I'm not attracted to an art piece because of its sexual implications. The erotic art I have is because of the culture it represents. Egyptians used the serpent prominently throughout their culture, and quite extensively. I collected the Egyptian pieces primarily because of the serpent." He smiled "The eroticism is an added bonus."

They watched as Sam rubbed his finger along the serpent images of the beautiful gold relief carving.

"The magic of the pyramids," he uttered softly.

"Pyramids?" Jenny had a puzzled look. "Did you say magic of the pyramids?"

"Yes," Sam reiterated. "We are fascinated by the art and culture of Egypt because these ancient people were so far advanced of all others in their form of communication and presentation. We still cannot even attempt to explain many of their accomplishments"

Sam glanced at Jessica, then Jenny. They were both truly enthralled; listening to his every word.

"Besides the serpents and their fascinating art, there is another aspect of Egyptian culture that I find very interesting. From ancient times, Egypt has been the cradle of magic and mystery. The magicians and the prophets were an inseparable part of their religion."

"Religion? Magicians and prophets? Doesn't that seem like a very peculiar mixture?"

"Peculiar, but true. That is actually recorded in our Bible. The dealings between the Hebrews and Egyptians, in many different situations in the Old Testament."

"Wow."

"The most powerful of all the religious figures in Egyptian society carried a scepter that had a serpent's head surmounted by the uraeus."

"What does that mean?"

"A scepter is a staff. A walking stick. Though it was used for many different purposes."

"What does surmounted by the uraeus mean?"

"Uraeus is a representation of the sacred asp of Egypt, Naja haje. It's the snake head that you see on the headdress of ancient Egyptian rulers. Their ultimate symbol of sovereignty."

"That little snake that looks like it's sticking out of the forehead of Egyptian kings?"

"Ah-h-h. That little snake is uraeus."

"What does surmounted mean?"

"The rod, or staff looks like a rigid snake, right?"

"Right."

"A large snake, with the head as the handle."

"Okay."

"Sticking out of the serpent's head, on the handle, is a very small snake, uraeus."

"Yeah, I think I have it, now."

"Good. Now, switching channels slightly . . . do you recall the story of Moses?"

"Moses? Sure."

"When Moses was trying to convince Pharaoh to release his people from slavery?"

"Yeah," Jenny chimed. "I remember all sorts of plagues and such before Pharaoh would agree to let the Israelites leave Egypt. And even something about snakes."

"Me, too." Jessica agreed.

Sam glanced at both girls. "Well, my favorite is the first confrontation. When Moses and Aaron went to Pharaoh and demanded that he release their people from slavery."

"Demanded?"

"That's right. The Lord told them to make it a demand. Aaron cast his rod upon the ground and it became a serpent."

"Right on. I do remember that."

"Do you recall what Pharaoh did?"

"No."

"Did he run like hell?"

"No. He summoned all the wise men and the sorcerers. As the Bible so aptly puts it, all the magicians of Egypt. They cast their rods also upon the ground, and every one of them became serpents as well."

"Wow. What happened then."

"Aaron's serpent swallowed up all the others."

"Ha! I guess that showed 'em."

"Yes, but it didn't sway Pharaoh in the least. He said it was just some magic trick."

Both girls were intrigued. "So, what happened?"

"Oh, you know the rest of the story. Moses was eventually able to convince Pharaoh to let the people go, and he led them out of Egypt. I just wanted to make a point about the serpent. I think that particular artifice was used for the first test because the serpent was sacred to the Egyptians, and the Lord felt it would cause great alarm."

"Sacred? That's why he used the serpent?"

"Definitely. There is constant conflict throughout the Bible between God and the serpent. In several places, reference is actually made to the worship of the serpent . . . by Israelites, not by the Egyptians."

"Is that true? In the Bible?"

"It's a fact. There's another interesting situation that I like involving Moses. It seems the snake situation became so bad that many people were dying from snake bites. The Lord told Moses to make a fiery serpent and mount it on a pole. He said that anyone who was bitten by a serpent could look upon the fiery serpent and be safe."

"Wow. That's crazy."

"Later in the Bible, there is another reference to that same fiery serpent. King Hezekiah had to destroy the bronze serpent Moses had made because the people had started to worship it. They called it their snake god, Nehushtan."

"I thought snakes, or serpents as you prefer to call them, represented evil."

"Yes. That is the most popular belief. The serpent of all ancient civilizations was considered to be the incarnation of the spirit of Evil."

"Then why did people worship them?"

"Most societies of ancient and primitive cultures worshiped those things that could cause them harm. They paid homage and made sacrifices to so-called gods to stay in their favor."

"So, the serpent they worshiped was evil?"

"Yes. The serpent symbolizes the ambiguous and eternal strength of Evil itself . . . Evil with a capital E."

"I understand eternal strength," Jessica acknowledged. "What do you mean by ambiguous."

"And by capital E?" Jenny interjected.

"Ambiguous simply means something that is often difficult to understand."

"You mean like people know what evil is, but don't really understand it?"

"Very good." Sam smiled. He was genuinely impressed. "I think in this case it actually means that evil is two-faced, or double-edged. You cannot always trust, that what you think you see, is what you actually see. That is truly ambiguous."

"Ah-so."

"Evil with a capital E. That simply means the ultimate evil. The Devil himself. There are devils, and then there is *The* Devil. Satan is THE Devil."

"Why are you so intrigued with the serpent? You must have hundreds of them in your house."

"Artistic. Mysterious. Symbolic. I've always been fascinated with the many different images of the serpent. I love tales of the dark ages, and the serpent is as prominent in those old stories as the knight himself. I started collecting dragons, and other serpent images and my interest grew from there."

"But," Jenny interrupted, "you said some of these have been in your family for many generations."

"True. Catch twenty-two. I'm not sure if any other people in my family were interested in the serpent symbolism, or if these artifacts with serpents are purely coincidental."

Sam hesitated a moment. "I think it is only fair to consider the Oriental concept as well."

Jessica's eyes lit up. "Oh yeah, the Chinese really have a thing for dragons, don't they!"

"You're right," Sam acknowledged. "In the far east, the dragons are considered to be angels . . . not demons. That's why you see the images of dragons prominently displayed in all their architecture. They burn incense and pray to dragons."

"To stay in their favor?"

"No, Jenny." Sam admonished. "They believe the dragons are magic. They control the elements of water and air, to produce rain, oceans, rivers; even the clouds, sky, and wind."

"Oh, wow!"

"Yeah, like Puff the magic dragon."

"Exactly."

When Sam gestured during that last explanation, the flash of his ring caught Jessica's eye. She grabbed his hand and took hold of his finger.

"Show Jen your ring, Sam." She pulled his hand forward and angled it toward Jenny. "You'll love this. It is absolutely the most fabulous ring I have ever seen in all my life."

Sam extended his hand, and Jenny took hold of his fingers. He pulled it back and took the ring off, and handed it to her. She rolled it over and over. It was indeed one fantastic piece of artistic jewelry.

"That is the ouroboros," Sam replied. "It's pure twenty-four karat gold I might add."

"Wow. It is absolutely spectacular." She turned it over and over, scrutinizing every intricate detail.

"The Ouroboros is the serpent which feeds on his own tail. It makes a complete circle and symbolizes the perpetual self-renewal of nature. That is the bona fide origin of what we now call the ring. And, we still use the ring to symbolize something that is never ending."

A noise attracted their attention. All three looked up to see Savannah standing in the doorway.

"You better come on, now! Mommy said she has to take Jenny home."

Sam looked directly at Jessica. "And no one even knows you're here, eh?"

Jessica jumped to her feet quickly. She smiled at Sam with all her innocence and then turned to face Savannah.

"Okay, Twerp. We're coming."

"Thanks, Sam. We have to go." She took Jenny by the hand. "C'mon Jen, we have to go."

"Nice meeting you, Jenny."

"Yeah, me too. Thanks for everything." She handed Sam the ring. "I really love all the dragons." She looked around, then back at Sam. "I would like to hear more about them."

"Anytime." He quickly added, "Just let me know a little bit in advance the next time."

Jessica took her friend's hand and pulled her toward the door. Jenny looked back as she was being dragged from the room and gave Sam a slight wave with her free hand.

Sam nodded and offered a waving gesture. He strolled into the bathroom, picked his towel off the floor, shook it, and hung it across the shower door.

He headed back toward the bedroom, stopped at the door, looked back and turned off the light.

He shook his head in disbelief, as he walked back into the bedroom. He surveyed the room full of serpents and smiled.

"Incognito," he muttered quietly to himself.

A devious smile crossed his lips.

Chapter 8

Sam pulled into the empty parking space closest to the clubhouse. He turned off the engine and visually surveyed the golf course. It was a beautiful day, in the mid-80s, but the sun was bright, and there were fewer than a dozen golfers on the exposed course in the middle of the afternoon.

Because of his friendship with Mike, Sam spent a lot of time at the golf course, but he really had no particular interest in the game itself. In fact, he had actually played only a couple of times in his entire life.

He gradually made his way out of the car and journeyed toward the clubhouse. After speaking to a few locals he met between his car and the porch, he stuck his head inside the door and looked the room over carefully.

Josh, a gaunt old gentleman in his 70s, was seated behind the counter reading a magazine.

The old man didn't even look up, not the slightest glance. Finally, Sam addressed the elderly gentleman.

"Afternoon, Josh. Is Mike around?"

The old man looked up from his magazine about half-way and pointed to a building about fifty yards down the blacktop path behind the clubhouse.

"He's down at the cart shed, charging golf carts."

Sam leaned back to look around the building toward the shed, then acknowledged. "Thanks."

He closed the door and ambled down the path. As he approached the structure, he spied Mike working on a golf cart in the far corner of the building.

Sam casually threw a hand into the air.

"Hey, Mike, whatcha doin?"

"Mil-dew-in," Mike exclaimed, "what's up?"

"I just stopped by to get that information about the people buried in the old cemetery across the road."

"Oh, yeah. I was looking at it last night. It's in the office." He moved around the cart, stood up and looked down the row, then at Sam. "Let me hook these last two carts to the charger, and I'll get it for you."

"Sure, no hurry. You go right ahead. Finish whatever you need to." Sam leaned over the cart to see where Mike was attaching the cord, then added as a follow-up afterthought, "I certainly don't want to interrupt a working man."

Sam turned to scan the room and immediately spotted a motorcycle in the opposite back corner.

He worked his way through the golf carts, toward the vehicle. "Hey, Mike," Sam exclaimed profoundly, "what's with the motorcycle?"

Mike stood and faced Sam and the bike. "That's my favorite toy," he replied. "I don't ride it anymore, but I can't bear to part with it. I keep it maintained, and that's about it."

""Wow! I'll say you keep it maintained. Looks to me like it's in perfect condition. Suzuki 450, that's what I had."

"No kidding? You had a motorcycle?"

"Sure did. Almost identical to this one. I really enjoyed riding, but I got rid of it several years ago. Don't ask me why."

He gently caressed the bike as Mike watched.

Mike, still wiping his hands, walked to the corner where Sam was gently rubbing the seat. "You're more than welcome to take her out . . . anytime you want."

Sam jerked around. Genuinely excited. "No shit? Now that sounds great . . . how 'bout this afternoon?"

"Why not, it'll do the ole girl good to have a run. I start her up ever so often, but I haven't actually been for a ride in quite a while."

"Evidently. I didn't even know you had it." Sam was getting excited. His mind flashed to the delight of freewheeling along the curvy rural back roads, flying with the breeze, swaying with

86

the curves, and simply enjoying the wondrous freedoms of nature. And this was one glorious afternoon for such a ride.

Mike fired back instantly. "Tell you what, let's clear a path and pull her outside."

Mike and Sam carefully retrieved the Suzuki from the shed and parked it on the path. As Sam cleaned off the dust, Mike cranked up the engine.

Sam straddled the bike, twisted the throttle a couple of times . . . varoom, va-r-o-o-o-o-m. He looked at Mike with an ear to ear grin. He was like a kid in a candy store.

"How about a helmet?"

"Oh, yeah. I've got a couple right in here." He darted into the shed and came back with two helmets. One in each hand. Looked at one, then the other.

"I like this one," Sam suggested, as he reached out to take a helmet from Mike.

"Try it on," Mike noted.

"Wow. Fits perfect." He looked at Mike. "I haven't had one of these on in quite some time. Feels great."

Mike then extended the other one toward Sam. "Take both, just in case you need a spare."

Sam looked up. Inquisitive.

Mike smiled. "You never know. You might see an irresistible hitch-hiker along the way."

Sam adjusted the helmet. It fit fine. He strapped the other one onto the luggage rack and was ready to roll. "See ya later."

Without hesitation, Sam headed up the path, threw a hand into the air as he turned around the clubhouse, then zoomed down the road and out of sight.

After enjoying an especially delightful ride through the back country, Sam came upon a quaint old country store deep in the gorge. He decided to stop and catch his breath and perhaps to even partake of a cold beverage.

He pulled up in front of the old store, parked the bike, took off his helmet and sauntered into the store.

Inside, he immediately spied a floor model soft drink cooler. Sam grabbed a ginger ale from the cooler and proceeded to the counter, where he began to converse with the cashier about absolutely nothing.

The experience brought back fond memories, and Sam was having a wonderful adventure.

The clerk was friendly and talkative. He listened attentively and nodded in response. Sam's bobbling head swung just enough for him to catch a fleeting glimpse of a delicate pastel form moving about the soft drink cooler.

He casually twisted around to get a better look, and saw an exquisite young creature with her lovely tush extending directly into his line of view.

His attention had been secured. Sam nonchalantly rolled his entire body around to get a better look.

A brief glance at her pretty face created a shiver of total excitement before she quickly tucked her entire upper torso into the beverage chest. Her petite waist rested gently against the edge of the opening, and she eased forward, raising both feet off the floor as she slid deeper and deeper into the big box.

The dainty silk-like fabric slithered seductively over her firm rounded physique, and Sam felt a very warm sensation flush throughout his entire body.

A sudden thought that the clerk was probably scrutinizing his every reaction, caused Sam to turn abruptly and reconstruct his composure. However, the clerk had gone to the other end of the room to assist some other patrons.

With no other impediment, Sam immediately returned his attention to the performance at the beverage cooler.

Her hand was now extended back toward him, holding a ginger ale. He looked around and didn't see anyone near, so he quickly strolled over and reached for the soft drink.

The delayed reaction caused her to twist around and peer out to determine why the bottle had not been taken from her grasp. She obviously didn't expect to see Sam.

Susie was an impeccable young creature, barely twenty-one. She was drop-dead gorgeous, sexy, with a sleek figure that would make any beauty queen jealous.

Sam held his hand toward the bottle.

She looked at his extended hand, then to his face. They made eye contact, and she bounced a sexy smile at Sam. Then, her provocative eyes moved slowly beyond him, as a slender, dainty hand reached around Sam to take the bottle from her outstretched hand.

"Now where did that come from?" he wondered.

Sam turned quickly to see who belonged to the exquisite hand. Virginia was 22, and just as beautiful as Susie, and quite well-endowed. She smiled at Sam. That brief glance caused an additional shiver of excitement.

Susie dived directly back into the cooler and came out with another drink. Sam looked about for Virginia. She had strolled around to the opposite side of the cooler. Just as Sam located her, she bent forward and placed her soda bottle into a slot to remove the cap.

When she leaned forward, a couple of wonderful secrets were revealed. Sam gazed down her loosely draped dress with utter delight. She obediently held the pose as she traded bottles with her friend.

Sam was caught in a weird sort of trance. She opened the other drink, looked up, and offered Sam a sumptuous smile.

Both girls were well aware that they had captivated his full attention. They were clearly turning him on, and he felt certain this show was strictly for him. They laughed quietly and talked to each other in low murmurs.

Sam could not hear one intelligible word, but really didn't care. His mind was in mute, and his total concentration was focused on the delightful view.

Much to his disappointment, Virginia stood erect, and he feared the show was over. However, to his astonishment, she slowly lifted the bottle in an upward arch and licked her lips with the very tip of her tongue.

She placed the round smooth edge of the opening against her lower lip and slid her tongue completely around the rim several times. She literally covered the entire top portion of the bottle in every conceivable manner. Then she tipped the bottle forward and stuffed her tongue into the small bottle opening.

Susie watched the activity intently. At this point, she reached forward and took the bottle from her companion. Curiously, she handed her own bottle to her friend and she continued to work on the one which had already been well tongued by her cohort.

She glided her hands feverishly over the bottle, and curtly manipulated her fingertips around the opening. She slowly put the bottle to her mouth, ran her moist tongue around the rim several times, and gradually maneuvered the protrusion inside her mouth.

Her full crimson lips gripped the glass tightly as the full neck of the bottle disappeared.

Sam felt a gentle touch on his shoulder.

Soft warm words in his ear asked, "Is that your bike sitting out front?"

Sam jerked his head around toward the voice, and his face was virtually touching Virginia's - nose to nose.

He was so completely captivated by Susie's performance, that he had not even seen Virginia come over.

She didn't wait for a response. "I love to ride motorcycles."

"You do?"

"Yes. I would do anything for a ride. The thought of all that power pulsating between my thighs simply drives me crazy."

"I can sure take care of that. Want to go for a ride?"

"You mean it? Right now?" She grinned and literally jumped up and down. "I sure would." Bubbling with excitement, she whirled around to her friend and exclaimed in a shrill voice, "Susie, I'm going for a motorcycle ride."

Susie instantly halted her performance and strolled over. She looked directly into Sam's eyes. "Follow me back to our camp," she suggested as she slowly turned her gaze to her friend, "and you can take me for a ride too."

Her bewitching eyes turned from Virginia to Sam, who was still staring at her.

Virginia looked sheepishly at Sam for approval. She gritted her teeth, waiting for a response. What could he say?

"Sure, that sounds great. I'm Sam, by the way."

Virginia extended her hand. "My name is Virginia." She held tightly to Sam's hand, and twisted around to acknowledge, "My friend is Susie."

Susie raised her hand delightfully, "Hi, Sam."

Virginia still had Sam by the hand. She turned, and gently pulled him toward the front door.

As they exited the building, Virginia let loose of his hand and rushed toward the motorcycle. She hurled her leg over the leather seat, and her agile fingers quickly grasped the hem of the delicate dress fabric.

Once on the seat, she pulled the dress to her crotch and tucked it securely under her bottom. She then ran her hands briskly along both sides to secure it tightly under her legs.

The swift action would normally have been fast enough to protect her precious modesty, but Sam was watching her very intently, and the glimmer of flesh acquired in the exact instant her leg swung high above the seat, stopped Sam dead in his tracks. Another fond memory to cherish the day.

That fleeting glimpse renewed the fantasies in his cluttered mind. He was still caught in an awkward trance but was able to clumsily hand her a helmet.

She graciously took the helmet, placed it on her head and pulled the strap under her chin. Then she realized Sam was frozen; standing there like a petrified log.

"I guess I should have waited?" she remarked with naive question in her voice.

"No." Her voice instantaneously snapped him out of the trance. "You're fine, I just wanted to make sure your chin strap is properly adjusted."

She smiled.

Sam slipped his foot judiciously across the seat in front of Virginia and eased into position. As he started the engine, her nimble fingers gently explored his chest, shoulders, and belly. She caressed him with sensitivity as he revved the engine and released the kickstand.

When he kicked the bike into gear and started off, she clutched him firmly with her left hand and wrapped her right arm across his chest. Her body rested snugly against his, and he could feel her breasts glide carelessly against his back. He became exuberant and stood erect with great interest.

The ride was magnificent but much too short.

Their camp was located just over a mile from the old store, in a peaceful setting on the river bank. Virginia glanced down as Sam stood up. His obvious pleasure caught her attention, and she literally beamed with a feeling of triumph.

"I'm so glad you enjoyed the ride," she replied. "I enjoyed it as well. Come, let me show you around."

"Do you camp here often?"

She took his hand and headed toward her tent. "We like to get away from the hustle and bustle of the city, and commune with nature . . . whenever we can."

"We leave all the stress of the real world behind." Susie's delicate voice cut sharply through the still air from another direction. "Just turn loose and have fun."

Sam swiftly turned around to see Susie sitting side-saddle on the bike. He did a hasty double-take, she was completely naked. As he gazed at the perfectly natural beauty, a feeling of complete unencumbered freedom flushed his senses. He could well appreciate their love for the back-to-nature attitude.

Susie clearly sensed his eyes upon her. She gently turned her head ever so slightly, in order to observe his reaction from the corner of her eye.

Virginia tugged, but detected Sam's strong resistance. She realized it was senseless to fight his urge. Virginia twirled about and kept talking as she calmly led Sam back toward his bike.

As they approached Susie, she whispered, "I have always dreamed of riding naked on a motorcycle."

She gleefully flipped her fingers through her hair to imitate the wind. "Of course, my companion should also be naked." She looked at Sam with a devious, extremely sexy grin.

"Take off those clothes; make my dream come true."

The fresh memory of his brief ride with Virginia blazed radiant in Sam's mind, and reckless illusions congested his head. Sam quickly undressed without a second thought.

Virginia knew Sam was now under Susie's control. She gently laid the palm of one hand against his chest and grasped him firmly, but gently with the other. She leaned toward his flushed face and spoke softly, "I'll be waiting for you to return."

She calmly pulled his face to hers and planted a warm, compassionate kiss, on Sam's unsuspecting lips. Then turned and walked toward her tent.

Sam watched her stroll away, as he put on his helmet. He looked at Susie and sighed. She giggled, sat up, and scooted back to give him room. Sam cautiously mounted the seat and started the bike.

The incomparable sensation of riding on a motorcycle naked, around the curvy, secluded, shaded mountain road, was unbelievable. That sensuous feeling of having seductive bare flesh snuggled magnetically against his backside very nearly terminated Sam's mortal existence.

The cool gentle breeze soothed his anxious flesh, and warm, enthusiastic fingers caressed his sensitive body. Every contour of the road brought another exquisite thrill.

Sam was caught in a dire dilemma; he wanted this ride to last forever; however, Virginia's words, *"I'll be waiting for you to return,"* kept running through his fragile mind. The haunting words excited him.

Reluctantly, he pulled to the side of the road to ask Susie if she was ready to return. Before he could get his helmet off, she leaned back on the padded seat and whimpered, "I've never made love on a motorcycle."

Sam grinned from ear to ear. A cold shiver rippled through his entire body, and he nearly went numb. He twisted around without hesitation and took advantage of the situation.

Susie fiddled with her hair as Mike was putting on his helmet. "Now that is what I call a great ride," she whispered.

They headed for the camp.

Susie slid off the rear of the bike and smiled delightfully at Sam. "Thanks for the wonderful ride," she recounted.

They looked around; there was no sign of life at the campsite. It was extremely quiet.

They walked to the tent.

Susie pulled back the tent flap, and Sam was staring at a beautiful nude vision reclined on a sleeping bag.

"Have a nice ride?" Virginia asked innocently.

"Exceptional," Sam replied.

"Well," Virginia said as she glanced at her friend and then back at Sam. "I think it's time to repay your kind hospitality."

She flashed a seductive smile.

Susie looked at Sam. She bit her bottom lip gently and smiled. She looked at Virginia.

Sam looked from one to the other, he couldn't believe this was actually happening.

Virginia extended her hand and beckoned.

Chapter 9

Sam strolled casually across the yard, to Carole's house, and rapped firmly on the kitchen door. The door opened ever so slightly and Carole greeted Sam.

She left the door open, as she turned away, "Come on in, Sam." Carole walked across the room toward the counter and extended her hand toward the table while she continued across the room. "Have a seat and I'll fix you a cup of java."

"Hi Nora," Sam greeted the guest. "Good to see you."

Nora, an attractive forty-year-old, was Carole's best friend. She and Carole met for coffee each day in order to keep each other abreast of all the news.

"Hello, Sam. What's up with you?"

Carole turned to interject. "Sam's taking Jess to Jackstown tomorrow. For a book signing."

Nora frowned with apprehension. "No! You're letting Jess go to Jackstown?" Her look was total dismay.

"Sure, she'll be with Sam. Besides, it's less than a hundred miles away. Jess has been begging to go with Sam on one of his autograph sessions for a long time, and this is the closest one he's had this year."

Sam detected the serious conflict in Nora's attitude. He decided to head off any potential problems. "We'll be at the Readmore Bookstores," Sam replied reassuringly. "They have three locations in the Jackstown area, and I'll be signing books for an hour at each store. Jess has been asking to go with me on a book signing for quite some time, and this seems to be the best opportunity."

"You can't be serious," Nora reiterated.

Sam was seriously confused by the reaction. He looked at Carole with uncertainty.

"Nora is concerned about the recent disappearances. The strange and mysterious activities in the gorge," Carole noted.

Sam was unquestionably relieved. "That explains why the atmosphere is so glum," Sam acknowledged, "but how does that affect my outing with Jessica?"

"Nora just told me about the two girls who disappeared in the gorge this weekend. They were her co-workers."

"Yes," Nora added quickly. "They were killed last weekend in the camping area toward Jackstown."

"What? I didn't hear about anyone getting killed."

"They're keeping it quiet," Nora admonished.

"Well," Carole admitted, "there is no real evidence the girls were actually murdered."

"Don't be silly, you know they were."

"Tell me about it," Sam requested.

Carole set a cup of coffee in front of Sam and took a seat at the table. Her expression was uncertain. No one said a word. Total silence. Sam was puzzled, he looked curiously from one to the other, and he realized Nora was just as much in the dark as he. He stared at Carole, then raised his palms upward.

"Well?"

Carole dropped her head. She looked up slowly. "I'm just not real sure how to say this."

Sam leaned forward. "For goodness sake, just spit it out, how difficult can it be?"

"Very difficult. It's about Jess."

Sam sat back, utterly shocked. "What does Jess have to do with two girls being murdered in the gorge?"

"Nothing at all." She looked up meekly. "This doesn't have anything to do with those girls. I've been trying so hard to figure this out and I want to get it off my chest . . . and perhaps you can offer some solution."

Nora took Carole's hands in hers. "Come on, tell us what's bothering you. Let us help, please."

Carole looked at Sam, then back at Nora. "It's an extremely delicate situation that I have here."

Sam was concerned. "Tell us about the problem. You know we'll do whatever we can to help."

"Jess is reaching that age where she wants to know more about her father."

Sam's relief was nearly obvious.

Nora quickly jumped in, "I know you don't like that good for nothing loser of a husband you had, but you're gonna have to let Jess find that out for herself."

Carole grimaced.

"Jess is a smart cookie," Nora added quickly, "she'll deal with it just fine, and you won't have to worry."

"That lousy S.O.B. I was married to, is not Jessica's father. He fathered Savannah, but not Jess."

Sam and Nora were both shocked. They looked at each other, then back at Carole.

"Jess doesn't know. Actually, nobody knows."

"You got that right," Nora exclaimed. "If Clyde Jackson isn't her father, who the hell is?"

Softly. "James Donovan."

A vision flashed through Sam's mind. A memory. He saw James Donovan coming out of the Hardware Store late at night. It was very dark in the alley behind the store. The young man was illuminated by a single 60-watt light bulb.

"Who the hell is James Donovan?" Nora asked.

Sam envisioned James fiddling with that big ring of keys, looking into the shadows, the smile of satisfaction when he finally locked the door.

"It was about fourteen years ago. We were young, and very much in love." She hesitated. "His parents owned the hardware store, Donovan's Hardware. We had big plans."

Sam remembered clearly. James stood up straight and turned around to face the ambiguous figure of a serpent. He could see the excruciating fear just before a brilliant flash of light ended the young life.

"What happened?" Nora was anxious.

"He disappeared. I knew he wasn't happy at home, but we were going to change all that, together."

Sam was solemn. Carole buried her face in her hands.

Nora consoled her. "It's okay, take your time."

"I figured he couldn't handle it, and just took off.

Sam was in a daze. He listened mutely.

"But, what about Jess?" Nora inquired.

"I found out I was pregnant a couple of days after James disappeared. That's why I married that bastard, Clyde Jackson. I know now that was a big mistake."

"You can say that again."

Sam frowned. He knew what was coming.

"It was bad enough if he had run away, as I first thought, but . . ." tears were forming. "They found James Donovan's bones in that grave over at Clear Creek."

"No-o-o."

Before anyone could say anything further, Carole looked at the clock, then the door, and immediately . . .

"Uh-oh, it's time for Jess. Let's get back to the girls in the gorge . . . quickly."

Nora couldn't believe her ears. "Wait just a minute! You can't leave us hanging like that."

Bam! The door swung open. They all looked to see Jessica come flying into the kitchen. She came bouncing across the room, beaming from ear to ear.

"Hey, Sam," she hailed with great enthusiasm. "Hi, Nora." She threw her arm around her mother's neck and gave her a polite peck on the cheek.

"Hey, Jess," Sam replied. "Ready for the big day?"

"You betcha," Jessica exclaimed radiantly.

Nora was still confused and exasperated.

"We'll need to leave by six a.m." Sam turned to Carole, "We should be back by six tomorrow night."

"Oh, I'll be ready," Jessica responded.

Carole looked at Jessica. "Sam's going to visit with us for a bit, sweetheart. Would you check on your sister for me? She didn't come in."

"Okay." Jessica turned, then looked back. "Nora, did you tell Sam about your friends?"

Carole was astounded. "How did you know that?"

Jessica was cavalier. "Everyone's talking about it."

"Honey," Carole replied comfortingly. "You know very well how everyone exaggerates."

"Yes," she looked at Sam with a smirk. "I sure do."

"Just the same," Carole insisted, "I'd prefer you didn't listen to our conversation."

"If I don't listen," with arrogance, "how will I know if you have all the latest details?"

"Whadda you mean?" Nora queried instantly.

Jessica threw a cunning sneer and retorted. "The kids at school bring in new information every day."

"More rumors and exaggerations," Carole replied, "being compounded upon exaggerations."

"Hey," Jessica replied smugly, "you just might be surprised. I have one classmate whose dad is Deputy Jasper Smith, another whose mom is Deputy Sadie Purdom, and, that nasty old newspaper woman's son, Jimmy Jacks is in my homeroom. I could go on and on . . . lots of credible informants."

"You think you're smart, don't you young lady?" Carole was quite agitated.

"C'mon Mom, you treat me like a baby."

Nora looked humbly at Carole. "What could it hurt? She probably knows more than we do, anyway."

Carole knew it meant a lot to Nora. She gave in reluctantly. "All right." She turned to Jessica. "But, if you have nightmares, young lady, I'll be very upset."

Jessica pulled a chair next to Sam. She bounced him a smile of complete and total victory.

Nora leaned forward and clasped her hands together.

"So, where were we?"

"I told Sam those two girls worked in the same office with you. And they came to the gorge just about every weekend."

"Yeah." Nora picked up the hint. "Last Monday neither of them showed up for work. That's not at all like either of them."

"So," Sam jumped in, "how did they determine they were actually missing from the gorge."

"The supervisor called their apartment several times. When he couldn't reach them by noon, a couple of the guys went to the apartment. No one was there. It was empty, but no sign of a struggle. Looked like they hadn't been there for quite a while."

"The police were notified," Carole added. "They eventually decided to check out their favorite camping area in the gorge."

"Their car was discovered at the campsite."

Sam had another vision. He saw deputies checking out the devastated campsite; examining the mess. The tent was still standing, and there were long vertical rips or cuts, indicating an attack or vandalism. He saw a deputy emerge from the tent, holding a shredded sleeping bag and ripped clothes.

"That's right!" Carole admonished. "The car was okay, but the tent, sleeping bags, clothing, and everything was literally shredded to bits."

"And the girls?" Sam didn't see the girls in his vision.

"No girls. But there was no indication of foul play."

"Whadda you mean no indication of foul play?"

"No blood. No signs of a struggle. You know, as far as murder, rape or anything. The camp was destroyed, and the car abandoned, but they don't know what happened to the girls."

Sam was ecstatic. "Their car was found abandoned, the two girls are missing, and their camp was torn to shreds?"

"They think some wild animals tore the camp apart," Carole added, "but what happened to the girls is a complete mystery."

"There was obviously foul play," Nora admitted. "But, there was no clue as to how the girls had disappeared. No sign of a struggle, or chase."

"How could there not be any sign of struggle, if the camp was torn to shreds."

A good question. When no immediate answer was offered, Jessica decided it was time to add her two cents worth.

"The way I heard it, there were lots of footprints, even some barefoot prints." She looked at each person individually for reactions, then continued, "all prints were clear, not like scuffs

100

caused in a fight, or even the type that would be created in a chase." Then an afterthought, "Also, even though the clothes were torn-up, it was like they had been jerked from the duffel bag and ripped apart, not like they were torn off the person. It was more like an animal rummaging for food."

"So, what sort of conclusions were determined by your sources, Jess . . . as to what actually happened?"

"They all concluded that the girls were not even present at the campsite when it was destroyed."

"Not there?" Nora exclaimed. "Where were the girls? And where the heck are they now?"

"No one knows?" Jessica shrugged. "Oh, but there were tracks from a motorcycle. They thoroughly searched a wide area, and found no sign of the girls."

"That's right," Nora reflected, "I remember now, someone saw the girls with a fellow on a motorcycle Saturday. That was the last time anyone saw them. Those tracks indicate the motorcycle was also at the campsite."

Sam was starting to feel uneasy. "Do they think the person on the motorcycle had anything to do with all this?"

"They obviously don't know much at this point, but it is within the Circle of Domain," Jessica added.

Everyone looked at her. Curious. "What circle of domain?" her mother asked.

"The Demon's Circle of Domain," she responded.

"The demon?" Nora shrieked.

"That's right," Jessica continued, "the demon is very much a suspect, given all the unusual circumstances."

"If the camp was all torn up, why do they think it was the demon? I thought the demon was neat," Sam asserted.

"Neat? How do you mean that?" Carole and Nora frowned and looked exasperated. Jessica smiled.

"Like neat and tidy." Sam shrugged. "Jess told me it was neatness that separated the demon from wild animals."

"Jessica told you that?" Carole was alarmed. She turned and glared at Jess.

A sheepish, yet guilty grin extolled her aura.

101

Jessica looked at Sam. "They don't believe the demon tore up the camp," Jessica explained, "they think that was done after the girls disappeared."

"If the Demon is their prime suspect, then they don't think the person on the motorcycle had anything to do with the girls' disappearance?" Sam emphasized.

"They figure he might have information that could help. He was obviously the last person to see the two girls alive."

"They don't know for sure the girls are dead," Carole said.

Everyone looked at her.

Jessica stared silently. "Anyway," she gradually continued, "they're looking for him. They just want to question him."

"They're looking for him?" Sam inquired.

"Yes. The clerk at the old country store near where the girls were camped said he left there with the girls. She described the man to the sheriff, but she didn't see the motorcycle."

"It's really a shame," Nora sighed. "Those girls were both so full of life, a virtual ball of energy."

"Evidently that was their downfall," Sam replied.

"Tommy Smith said his dad checked to see if there were any new bones in that grave at Clear Creek."

Everyone looked at her and waited. Finally. "Well?"

"Nope! No new bones. Sheriff McNeal figures the demon has another hiding place."

Sam glanced at his watch. "I'd best get back to the house," he remarked. He stood and slid the chair under the table.

As Sam made the short walk to his house, he pondered the information which had been offered. He knew the police were looking for him and wondered if he should turn himself in.

What would happen if he didn't go in voluntarily, and they were to discover that he was the person on the motorcycle?

He strolled. He thought. He reached the house, took the doorknob and stood for a brief moment.

He shrugged his shoulders and went inside.

Chapter 10

Sam stepped outside and looked at the beautiful morning sky. He stretched vigorously, then placed his hands on his hips to arch his back. He looked at the sky as he inhaled the brisk morning air deep into his lungs.

Sam dearly loved the fresh clean air of the early mountain morning. He stood by the car as he surveyed the area around his house. His scanning perusal caught a glimpse of the trees which lined the river.

He slowly walked toward the front of the house and looked over the bank at the Winding River, which flowed nonchalantly past the edge of his property.

"Hey, Sam," Jessica yelled as she came hoofing rather hurriedly down the driveway with her mother.

Sam turned and watched them approach.

"Hope I'm not late."

"You'd think she was getting ready for the Prom," Carole noted. She shook her head in utter disbelief.

Jessica cast a disapproving glare at her mother.

"No," Sam casually checked his watch. "You're not late at all. Right on time."

Jessica placed her arms on her waist and twirled about. "Do I look okay."

Sam smiled. He could see what Carole meant.

"No."

Inconceivable shock.

"You look much better than okay. I'll have to say you look very beautiful. Very beautiful, indeed."

Jessica's dismay turned immediately into a smile. "I wasn't searching for any pseudo-compliments."

"That's good, because you didn't get one."

"I told her she did not have to be so particular. You would think it was her book signing."

"I want to look good," Jessica scowled. "You don't want Sam to be ashamed of me, do you?" She stared at her mother with obvious aggravation.

"There's no chance of that," Sam replied quickly. "But you really do look great, just the same. I will be very proud to have you escort me. In fact, I might just let you stand in for me."

Jessica laughed. "Thanks. Do I sign your name or mine."

"Mine for now," Sam raised his eyebrows, "and probably yours some day very soon."

Jessica smiled and looked at her mother.

Sam checked his watch again.

"I can take a hint," Jessica declared.

Sam walked toward the car. "Yep. I suppose we had better hit the road, or neither one of us will be signing any books."

Jessica ran around and jumped into the passenger seat. Carole strolled over to Sam. "Be careful."

"We will," Sam assured her. "Don't worry, I'll take good care of her. We'll be back by six. I'll phone if there's a change."

Carole stood back. Sam got into the car. She bent down to wave at Jessica and continued to wave as they backed out and drove up the hill.

"So," Sam asked, "how's your friend, Jenny?"

Jessica shrugged. "She's okay."

"Is she still talking about monsters?"

"Everyone's talking about monsters and demons, but at least Jenny doesn't think it's you anymore."

"Well, that's good news?"

"Yeah, she thinks you're cool."

"Cool, huh?"

"That's right. Don't get the big head, but she was really impressed with you. She keeps asking me when I'm going to bring her back to learn more about the dragons."

Sam pressed his lips together and nodded. "So we can say your mission was accomplished, then?"

"Definitely. She even defends you now, if anyone else calls you a monster. But none of the kids are saying that anymore."

"The kids?"

"Right. The kids don't think you're the devil."

"Does that mean their parents still think I'm the Demon of Clear Creek?" Sam smiled.

Jessica squinched her mouth. "Some of 'em do."

"Well, that should change soon."

"Whadda you mean?"

"You'll see. Time and circumstances always have a way of healing most things."

Sternly. "Don't keep any secrets from me, Sam."

"No secrets from you. You said that newspaper woman was the primary accuser, right?"

"Yeah, that's right."

"I just have this strange feeling that she will have a change of attitude before long. Just a feeling."

"I certainly hope your feeling is correct."

With his curiosity adequately satisfied, Sam engaged Jess in superfluous small talk for the rest of their trip.

As they drove through Jackstown, they witnessed a most unusual stir of activity along the streets. When they pulled into the parking lot of the Readmore Bookstore, they noticed people milling, talking, whispering. Sam and Jessica were curious.

Jessica looked at Sam. "Wonder what's going on."

"I don't know," Sam replied, as he pulled into a space near the entrance. He looked around. "Something is certainly awry."

They got out of the car and headed toward the bookstore, still looking around, catching some curious glances.

Sam opened the door and let Jessica enter first. As he followed her into the store, he saw the manager, looking out the window. He turned and looked back toward the parking lot.

"What's going on?" Sam inquired.

The manager walked to him with her hand extended. "Hello, Mr. Pent. So glad to have you, here. People really love your books." She looked at Jessica, "And who is this pretty young lady you have with you ?"

Sam placed his hand gently on Jessica's shoulder. "This is my friend, Jessica. She's my sidekick for the day."

"Very nice to have you as well, Jessica." She turned and looked out the window. "We were expecting a big crowd, today, but now I'm afraid it could well be a little disappointing."

"What's going on?" Sam repeated.

"We have a table set up for you over here." She led them toward a nice table with a variety of his books displayed on top. They followed but were waiting patiently for an explanation. She motioned toward the table and then turned to face Sam. "A group of Jackstown teenagers has disappeared."

"Disappeared?" Sam looked at Jessica, then out the front window, before returning his attention to their host.

"Yes, it's terrible?"

Sam and Jessica nodded in agreement.

"Everyone has been talking about those two girls who disappeared in the gorge last week. Now six of our own children have gone missing."

"Please, tell us about it."

"There's not much to tell. They're missing. All at once."

"Surely there's more to it than that," Sam insisted.

"This morning Mrs. Walper realized that her twelve-year-old daughter, Kathy, was not at home. She called the best friend, Bonnie. When Bonnie's mother went to her room to see if she knew where the Walper girl might be, she wasn't there. It kept on like that until we found that there were at least six missing children, and not a single clue as to where they might be, or what might have happened. Someone said it was just like all the mysterious goings on in Culver City."

Sam and Jessica looked at each other.

"Perhaps you should write a book about all the strange occurrences in the gorge."

Sam smiled.

"That's a great idea," Jessica concurred.

The manager turned and walked away.

Sam sat at the table and fiddled with the book display. It turned out to be quite a successful day, in spite of the uneasy apprehensions.

Evidently most people weren't swayed by the disappearance of the teens, but nearly every visitor did mention the tragedy.

As the time for his personal appearance at the third store drew to a close, Sam signed a few extra copies of each book and announced he was ready to leave.

When they got into the car, he looked at his watch and asked Jessica, "Are you ready to head home?"

"I'm with you," she responded.

"He checked his watch one more time and calculated quickly in his head. "Well, if you don't have anything else you need to do, I'd like to stop by the gorge on our way back."

A look of surprise crossed her face. "The gorge?"

"Yes. I have an idea where those missing teens might be."

"You do?"

"Yes. Everybody had been talking about those missing girls, and they probably looked for the missing teens around that same campsite." He looked at Jessica. "But I have a feeling they might be near Satan's Peak."

"Satan's Peak?" There was alarm in her voice. "Why do you think they're near there? No one dares to go around that area."

"Remember discussing Miss Susie?"

"The mummy?"

"The same. Mike told me that she was found in a cave near Satan's Peak. Those missing kids went looking for something."

"Looking for something?"

"That's right. Either the missing girls, or the demon."

"Why Satan's Peak?"

"I think Satan's Peak was their destination since it is most likely the only place they would need to sneak off to visit."

"Hmmm. You may be right."

"I have been listening to comments all day, and the more I heard, the more obvious it became. They slipped off without a word because they knew they could not get permission. So, where would that be?"

"Satan's Peak!" Jessica exclaimed. She was excited. "Okay, let's do it. I've never been to Satan's Peak."

Sam raised his eyebrows. "Not many people have," he acknowledged, "and it's on our way back to Culver City."

They came to the curvy mountain road and the turn-off for the gorge. As they pulled off the gravel road into the camping area parking lot, they saw a bunch of bicycles near the path.

Jessica pointed to the bikes at once. "You're right," she exclaimed. "Look at those bikes."

Sam smiled. He parked close to the bicycles. They got out of the car, and walked over, looked briefly at the bikes, and then began to survey the surrounding area.

"Gracious! Where do we begin?"

"Well," Sam replied. He pointed toward the path. "The cave is down that way. Let's look there."

Their eyes searched the woods on both sides as they strolled down the narrow mountain path. Soon they heard the faint sound of voices. They stopped for an instant to listen, then picked up the pace.

When they rounded the hillside, Jessica and Sam observed some commotion near the entrance to the large cave. They watched closely, and then hurried toward the immense clearing where the activity was taking place.

A group of kids was arguing with a man. Some were even struggling with him. Sam and Jessica could only see the man's back, but the teens appeared to be in trouble. Sam could only remember one name, so he called it out loud.

"Bonnie?"

"Kathy!" Jessica screamed.

Everyone looked toward the sound. The old man held a walking stick in one hand and grasped the arm of one teen with the other.

"Hey there," Sam yelled. "What's going on?"

The man looked up, let loose of the girl, and ran down the path toward the river.

The group of kids came running to meet Sam and Jessica. They were excited and clearly shaken. They didn't know these people from Adam, but it was the jubilant ambiance of a family reunion. They had actually been rescued.

"You saved our lives." Kathy rattled off, fast and furious. "My name's Kathy Walper." She looked at her friends. "We're from Jackstown. We came here looking for those two girls who disappeared last weekend."

"Slow down, you're safe. My name is Sam Pent. This is Jessica Jackson. We came here looking for you."

Surprise flushed their faces. "Looking for us?"

"That's right. The whole town has been searching for you everywhere. Your disappearance has caused quite a turmoil."

"Hey, you're the famous author," Bonnie pointed.

The others looked at her.

"You know," she explained. "Sam Pent. He was supposed to autograph books at the Readmore today."

They all looked at Sam.

"I did. That's where we heard about you kids."

"Yeah," Jessica added with excitement. "Everyone thinks the Demon got you."

The teens looked at each other in amazement.

"I think he almost did," one boy explained. "You saved us from the Demon."

"I don't think that was the Demon," one girl said. "I think they saved us from a scroungy old hermit."

"But he was trying to force us into that desolate old cave," Bonnie added.

"If he was the Demon," the girl continued, "he probably would have taken them as well."

"She makes a good point," Sam replied. "Whether it was actually the Demon or not, we'd better let your friends and families know you guys are safe. I have a phone in my car, let's head back to the parking area."

"We got lost in the woods, way down that path," Bonnie explained. "We wandered around for hours. That old man appeared out of nowhere and showed us the way back here."

"But, he wouldn't let us go any farther," Kathy insisted. "He tried to take us into that cave."

"Wonder why?" Sam asked. He looked into the mysterious darkness. "There's nothing in there."

"He didn't just appear," another boy added. "I felt someone watching us all day."

"Yeah, me too," came another voice, "it was truly an awful . . . eerie, feeling."

"You're right," Kathy remarked. "There is nothing in that old cave. We explored it when we first got here."

"You went into the cave?" Jessica asked excitedly.

"Yeah," Kathy admitted. "It got dark just past the entrance. We didn't have any light, so we didn't go in very far."

"But we could tell there wasn't anything in there," Bonnie replied. "We yelled and listened. We really listened carefully."

"And there weren't any fresh footprints."

"Footprints?" Sam inquired.

The fellow turned to him. "Yes. The floor of the cave is very soft and impressionable, especially in the mouth of the cave." He pointed into the cave. "All the way back to that little stream."

"Well," Sam insisted. "We had better get moving."

They reached the parking lot. "Give me a number," Sam said. "We'll call your parents to let them know you're okay. I can crowd all of you into my car and we'll have someone come pick up your bicycles."

"My dad has a van," Kathy replied.

"My dad can bring his truck for the bikes," Bonnie added.

They called, and the decision was made that the van and truck would come if Sam and Jessica could wait with the teens. Sam called Carole and explained the situation. He told her they might be a little late, but that everything was okay.

The teens made Sam out to be a hero when their folks arrived. After the details had been straightened out, Sam and Jessica headed home with a feeling of satisfaction.

Carole, Savannah, and Nora were all waiting at the house, anxious to hear all about the big adventure. Jessica filled them in with all the intricate details, and Sam inserted vital bits and pieces, every now and then.

Chapter 11

All of Culver City was abuzz with the heroic deeds of a local celebrity, Sam Pent. In fact, the entire state was proclaiming him a hero, and the story even made the national news.

Headlines read:

"Sam Pent Rescues Jackstown Teens" Front page news, even for the *Culver City Beacon*, and the articles each included a photo of Sam and Jessica with the rescued teenagers.

Of course, there was no mention of any demon in any of the articles, just that they had been rescued from the gorge, where they had been lost.

Then came the big headline:

"Governor to Award Medal to Sam Pent"

Plans were being made for a special celebration, during which the mayor would cite Sam for his humanitarian services, and the Governor would award him the Medal of Honor. It was perhaps the most exhilarating activity to hit this community in many decades - maybe ever.

News clips of Sam, Jessica, and the teens continued to run daily on television stations across the state, most of the time attached to a new interview with Sam and some dignitary who wanted to get in on the action.

Sam Pent had been transformed, instantly, from a possible monster to a local hero. And the fact that he was credited with saving six Jackstown teens from the very same demon he had so frivolously been accused of being just days earlier, was not only ironic but most exceptional.

All his friends were very pleased with this new revelation.

Jeri Jacks, one of the remaining skeptics had been placed in the precarious position of planning the celebration banquet. The Mayor asked the Woman's League to be in charge of this important function, and as Chairman of the League, Jeri was responsible for the preparations.

Personally, Jeri still considered Sam Pent as the number one suspect, not merely as a serial killer, she actually believed he was some monster; even the devil himself.

Her influence over others in this particular situation had instantly faded, and she was very much alone in her persuasion. She knew it would be professional suicide to persist with her personal convictions at this point in time. Reluctantly, she would perform to the best of her abilities.

Jeri sat quietly at her desk, diligently drafting the necessary lists, Sheriff McNeal suddenly appeared.

"Change your mind about Sam Pent?"

Jeri offered a look of outright disgust. She knew she had to be cautious, but felt she could trust the sheriff. "Not likely," she responded indignantly. She looked up, laid her pencil on the pad, and continued. "It's like a puzzle where the pieces all fall into place too conveniently. Simply too good to be true."

"I know what you mean," the Sheriff added, "but all the pieces have not yet fallen into place."

"Are you sure? Sam Pent was the only true suspect in a catastrophic mystery, and then all of a sudden, all those unexplained things which made him a suspect are curiously revealed, or appropriately covered up."

"For instance?"

"Books. Remember you asked about his published work? You asked me if he was such a famous writer, didn't he have any books . . . now, all of a sudden . . . for the first time that I can substantiate, he holds an autograph session within a one hundred mile radius of Culver City. And guess what? He's a well -known celebrity there."

"Curious perhaps, but quite possibly a mere coincidence. There is no indication it was intentional, and nothing to prove any sort of cover-up."

"I honestly feel that a month ago there was no one in Jackstown who even knew his name. And a hero!?"

"For saving six Jackstown teenagers."

"More precisely, for saving six children who were in the gorge looking for two victims of his own handiwork. And," she acknowledged vehemently, "he just happened to have a witness from Culver City with him for the miraculous rescue."

Sheriff McNeal offered a half-hearted laugh and looked at Jeri. "You'd better ease up or you're gonna have a stroke."

"Why did six teens from the exact same town where Sam was headed, go looking for two girls that none of them knew? Why was this the only time Sam had a witness with him?"

Jeri jumped to her feet straight away, gritted her teeth and slammed her fist onto the desk. "Why am I, the only person who still thinks Sam Pent is a monster, put in the position of having to publicly acknowledge that he saved those teens from the demon . . . the same demon I know he is?"

The Sheriff laughed. "Irony. Coincidence. Call it what you like, but if you keep stressing like this, I guarantee you're gonna blow a gasket. Don't worry about it, Jeri. If all your suspicions are correct, you'll surely come out on top in the long run."

"Thanks, Sheriff. But it really grates my craw."

She sat down and clinched her fists.

"I don't know what to tell you. I think the demon is keeping a step ahead of us, whether or not it is Sam Pent. We have to keep our heads, and prove we are smarter than a demon."

"He might be a lot more than a common old demon," Jeri exclaimed. He's aware of what we know, and even knows what we're going to do next."

"It sure does seem like it." He paused. "So, how's the big event taking shape?"

"It should be quite a spectacle. The Governor and the Mayor will be vying for the spotlight, but the real winner in all this will obviously be that damned dark creature from beyond."

"Jeri, I think there's something you should know."

"And what is that?" Jeri inquired.

"The Governor had already planned to award the Medal of Honor for Humanitarian Services to Sam Pent."

He paused briefly. "Before he saved those teenagers in the gorge. That incident just added icing to the cake."

Jeri looked at the sheriff. "That may be true, Sheriff. But, I'll bet my last dollar the decision was not made before I revealed all that information to you about the Pent generations."

The sheriff was thinking deeply.

"I'll tell you something else," Jeri rationalized. "I bet Sam Pent knew he was going to receive the Medal of Honor before the Governor did."

"Do you think Sam knows that you provided me with that extraordinary information about his family?"

"I most certainly do. I believe he knows a lot more than we realize. Like you said, nothing can be proven, but I know it's all true." She hesitated. "I'm afraid I caused all this clamor."

"How's that?"

"Well, since you didn't have any proof, I thought I could force him to make a mistake, by talking it up all over town. I'm afraid I just gave him forewarning."

"I'm aware of the rumors. That was definitely not a smart move. However, at this juncture, you're likely the only person in this county, who doesn't consider Sam Pent to be a hero. You best keep your accusations to yourself."

"The only one?" Curious. "Does that count you out?"

"Oh, don't count me out just yet. I have to remain objective for professional reasons, and I never reach conclusions until there is enough evidence to charge someone with a crime. But, I have learned to keep my personal feelings in check, that's why I can suggest for you to do the same. Be patient."

"Good. Just keep an open mind, I'll settle for that."

"Fair enough. I better be moving along, and let you get back to planning your festivities." He grinned.

"Is there some special reason for this visit?"

"Yes, and I think I covered everything."

Jeri stared at him.

He didn't offer any further explanation.

Sheriff McNeal left, and Jeri reluctantly returned to her task of organizing committees for the ceremony.

Jeri knew this had to be absolutely the best celebration she could arrange. Her professional reputation was at stake. This was an extremely important function for Culver City. It was the first time in history a Governor had made a visit here, and on this special occasion he would honor one of its own citizens.

She also knew the sheriff was right; it was very important that she keep her personal feelings to herself. At least for now.

Everyone was talking about Sam saving the teens, and the awards being heaped upon him. He was their hero, and the whole town was filled with pride. Sam's brave deed reflected positively on the entire community, and everyone was basking in his glory. Sam had made this small town famous.

Jessica had also become a celebrity. All of her classmates constantly grilled her about the adventure.

The thought of Sam's remark, *"Sign my name, for now, yours someday soon,"* kept popping into her head. It was probably just a coincidence. Anyway, the memory of the day made her very happy.

Jenny exhibited a more sincere interest in Jessica's day with Sam than with actually finding the lost teens.

Jessica and Jenny were walking home from school. They were strolling along the road by the golf course, when Jenny suggested, "I guess no one thinks Sam is a monster, now."

"You got that right," Jessica admitted with glee. "I don't think anyone remembers ever calling him a monster."

"Yeah. I heard that newspaper woman who spread all those nasty rumors is planning the banquet in Sam's honor."

"And you know what?" Jess jumped with excitement, "Sam has insisted that I get an award too; and I didn't do anything."

Jenny squealed. "You're kidding!"

"No, it's supposed to be a secret. Sam says we both found those teens, and that I should share the glory."

"That's true. You both did find them."

"Not really. It was all his idea to go to the gorge looking for the kids. I was just along for the ride."

"Just the same, don't you feel sorta special?"

A shy grin, followed by a shrug. "Yes. In a way."

Jenny squealed again. "I'm so excited!"

"Truthfully," Jessica took both Jenny's hands and looked at her with a teeth-gritting grin. "I was much more excited about going to Satan's Peak. I didn't even think about the kids."

"Well, I'm glad it all happened. I like everyone thinking he's a hero instead of a monster."

"Yeah, Sam said they would."

Instant curiosity. "Whadda you mean he said they would?"

Jessica stopped and thought about what she had just said. "Well, he actually said, that everything would soon change."

"I still don't understand, what does that mean?"

Jessica slipped into a state of deep concentration. She wanted to remember the situation precisely. "I told Sam some people still considered him to be the demon causing all the trouble. He smiled and told me not to worry," she paused, "that would all change, soon. Those were his exact words."

"Well, he was certainly right."

"Yeah . . . outer limits weird."

They approached the side road where they would part ways. Jenny headed up the road and waved to Jessica, who continued on the main road toward her house.

Jessica darted quickly across the yard and popped into the kitchen, with her usual vim and vigor.

Carole and Nora were seated at the kitchen table, having their coffee, and afternoon chat.

Jessica listened intently for a moment before entering their conversation, "Are we discussing the big event?"

"Yes, little Miss Hero, isn't everybody?" Nora smiled at Jess.

"Hello, sweetheart," Carole greeted.

Jessica replied curtly, "Well, I do believe the whole town's talking about me . . . and Sam."

"You sure have developed an attitude, "Carole replied.

"It's okay," Jessica remarked. "I'm just excited about Sam being a hero . . ."

"Sam!" Nora interrupted. "And how about Miss Jess?"

She laughed. "There's more commotion over this, than there was about finding that grave full of bones on Clear Creek."

116

"That's a good thing. We never have enough good news. I think it's time to cause a commotion over some good deed rather than about a terrible tragedy."

"Yeah," Nora chided, "It certainly is causing a great deal of excitement. Sam's getting a lot of attention."

"Yep. He sure is."

Carole noted sadness in her voice. "It's okay, sweetheart. Everything will back to normal soon."

"I feel kinda weird," Jessica conceded. "And I can't really explain what I mean."

"It's natural, honey." She wrapped her arm around Jessica. "It's a combination of confusion and jealousy."

"Jealousy?" Jessica pulled back hastily. "Hey, I might be confused, but I'm certainly not jealous. Do you really think I am jealous of the attention Sam is getting?"

"Not in the way you took it. It's just that you had him all to yourself before he became a hero."

She frowned. "I'm just concerned, that's all."

"Concerned? Well, don't be. All the attention in the world won't change Sam's feelings toward you."

"Things might not get back to normal anywhere too soon," Nora noted deliberately.

Carole and Jessica looked at her. "Take the big celebration, for instance," Nora said, "the original plan was to hold the award ceremony in front of City Hall and then have a banquet at Benny's Place. Well, it seems everyone wants to attend the banquet, so they'll present the awards at the banquet, which means they had to move the location to some place that would hold more people. When they finally realized the only place that would hold all the people who want to attend the activities is the school gym, they changed locations again."

Carole insisted, "Take my word for it, everything will be back to normal before you know it."

Nora raised her eyebrows and turned her head to one side in disbelief. "We'll see."

"Speaking of the banquet," Carole attempted to change the focus, "We will be guests of honor."

"Me too?" A shrill excited voice came out of the frisky little twerp who scampered into the room and wrapped both arms around her mother's leg.

"Yes, Savannah, you too."

"All my friends want to know what it's like living next door to a big famous hero." Savannah blurted.

"And what do you tell them," Carole asked.

"Oh, I tell them Sam is just an ordinary hero. That I really like him, and we do lots of things together."

"Yeah?" Nora questioned.

"Yeah, and they all get really excited. They want to know everything, all the details."

As Jessica listened to her little sister, she realized that was exactly the same sort of experience she was having. Perhaps her mother was right. All the unusual feelings and concerns may be caused by this wealth of attention all of a sudden being heaped upon Sam.

She was no longer having to defend Sam and wondered how all this was affecting him. He always took things in stride. Nothing seemed to bother him, and somehow he knew this was going to happen.

"Of course," she thought to herself, *"Sam should be used to the attention. He was already a celebrity."*

Even though this would be the very first time the Governor had been to Culver City, Sam had rubbed elbows with several governors. It was all a part of his normal life.

Jessica recalled Sam's reaction to the people who came to see him at the bookstores. He was very polite, very congenial, but he took it all in stride.

She was very excited, but it was just another day for Sam.

It was definitely time for Sam to be honored in his own hometown, and not because he saved those teens, but that was as good an excuse as any.

Chapter 12

There were two extravagant celebrations held annually in Beckham County. The Lions Club's Fourth of July Fireworks Display, and Culver City Ice Cream Social held in October. The Ice Cream Social was a special project of the Beckham County Homemakers Association.

The county's population always began to swell a week prior to each activity, and nearly doubled for the actual weekend of the festivities. It slowly returned to the normal size within a week following each event.

The Golf Tournament that Jasper pinpointed, was not an annual event and didn't bring in near the capacity of bodies as the Fireworks Display. The Ice Cream Social didn't fit within his Demon guidelines time wise.

Jasper had decided the Fireworks display was the most obvious target for the Demon's renewal endeavor.

Preparations for the Fourth of July celebration had been underway for several weeks. The committee and workers who were striving to achieve a successful project seemed to be unaware of any threat or danger from the evil supernatural power that was lurking about Beckham County.

The big day had finally arrived, and no one had seemed at all concerned about any possible dangers from the evils of a natural or supernatural serial killer.

On the afternoon of the fireworks show, Sam was relaxing comfortably on his front porch, enjoying the serene waters of Winding River, which flowed in front of his secluded cabin.

He was totally mesmerized.

The sound of Savannah skipping happily down his gravel driveway broke into Sam's state of hypnoses. He looked up as she approached. It was an all too familiar sound, and he had no doubts who the perpetrator might be. He watched amusingly, as she nonchalantly skipped across the yard.

"Hey, Sam." She threw up a hand.

"Hello, Savannah. How's my girl?"

"Fine, how 'bout you?"

Sam shrugged. "Can't complain. What have you been up to? I haven't seen much of you lately."

"Me and Jess have been watching 'em build benches for the big fireworks show."

"Oh, you have? Isn't the big show tonight?"

"Ye-e-ep. It's gonna be like a carnival. All kinds of games, music, rides, and stuff."

"Sounds like fun, but if they don't finish building those bleachers pretty soon, it will be too late."

"Oh, Sam." She batted her hand through the air. "You're so silly. Besides, they're 'bout done."

"Well then, have you reserved your seat for the show? You want to be able to see everything."

She frowned. "There ain't no reserved seats. We'll get there in plenty of time to get a good seat. Mommy said so. I'm posed to ask you to go."

"What time are you going?"

"I don't know for sure, but there's a whole lot of things to do there before the fireworks."

"What sort of things?"

"I said it's going to be like a carnival. You know, all kinds of games, music and that sort of stuff."

"Sure does sound interesting."

"So, are you going with us?"

"We'll see."

"What does that mean, we'll see?"

"That means I'm not sure . . . maybe."

"Maybe!" She shook her fist in determination. "I want you to go with us. I'll be very mad if you don't."

"I know better than that. You won't get mad at me. Besides, what if I don't want to stay as long as you?"

"Oh, you will. It'll be lots of fun." She looked up and pursed her lips. "Anyway, we're going to walk, so you can come back anytime you want."

"Okay, I'll see."

"Sam! I really will be mad if you don't go with us." She puffed out her lower lip, squared her feet, and firmly placed her clinched fists on her hips.

Sam ignored her obstinate attitude. "It looked to me like they're building the bleachers at the edge of the old cemetery, across from the golf course."

"Yeah. So what? What's that got to do with anything?"

"Just seems like it'd be pretty scary sitting in that spooky old graveyard after dark."

She was totally relaxed. "They don't want people too close to the fireworks. You can see better from up there. And I won't be scared; there'll be lots of people."

"How about the people who disappeared?"

"Sam. Are you trying to scare me?"

Before he could respond, they were distracted by a rustling noise coming from the road. Both of them jerked around and looked toward the driveway.

"Uh-oh," she clinched her teeth. "I'm in trouble, now."

"*In* trouble? You *are* trouble."

"Sam!" She swatted his arm. "I am *not* trouble."

Jessica hailed a greeting. "Hey, Sam."

"Hey, Jess. Hello, Carole."

"We've been waiting for you," Carole replied.

"Waiting?" Sam looked at Savannah. "Trouble?"

Savannah gritted her teeth and looked at Sam with raised eyebrows. "I came to get you, 'member?"

"Yes," Carole explained, "We're ready to go."

Sam looked at the afternoon sky. "It's much too early for a fireworks display?"

"Cheeze," Savannah plopped her signature clinched fists firmly on her hips. "I told you there was lots of things to do."

Savannah looked at Carole. "I already told him. He's just too doggone stubborn."

"Come on, Sam," Carole purred seductively. "You will enjoy it, and it'll make the girls very happy."

"Yeah," Savannah spouted excitedly, "It'll make us so very happy, Sam."

"I had planned to stay in tonight."

Jessica took his hand. "It'll do you good." She tilted her head and flashed her charming smile. "Ple-e-a-a-s-e-e."

Carole stared at Sam, "Are you okay?" She leaned forward, "You look a little peaked."

Sam was taken back at this abrupt change of direction. "Yes. Maybe a little languid, but I should be rejuvenated and ready for bear by tomorrow."

"He's okay, Mommy." Savannah tugged fiercely at Carole's arm. "Make him go with us."

Sam looked down. He knew he could not deny Savannah and Jessica. "Okay, give me a minute."

Sam went into the house and was back in a flash. He pulled the door shut. Savannah grabbed one hand, Jessica took the other and extended her other hand toward Carole. The four of them moseyed up the road toward the golf course.

It was indeed a treat for Sam. He enjoyed walking and talking, laughing and joking. His original plans for this evening had now been completely disrupted. His priorities had quite unexpectedly become totally flip-flopped.

As the golf course came into view, Sam's attention was suddenly diverted. He became solemnly quiet and stared at the sight ahead. There was an exceptionally large number of law enforcement personnel. He surmised all the county contingent was on hand, plus ten, possibly twenty or more, state troopers.

Carole felt his observation. She looked to see what had distracted him, then focused on the scene which had captured his attention.

"Wow," she exclaimed. "I certainly hope there are no crimes committed in any other part of the county tonight." She looked around. "Make that anywhere in the entire state."

"I don't think I have ever seen such a grandiose collection of toy cops," Sam remarked.

Carole laughed. "That's a good one."

"Yeah." Sam laughed. "Just when you almost think they're real, they do something dumb to let you know they aren't."

They both laughed.

"What's so funny?" Jessica looked up at Carole.

"It's nothing, Honey," Carole muttered softly. "We're just laughing. That's all."

"Hey, Sam!" Mike yelled.

The familiar voice collared their attention, and all four of them looked toward the Clubhouse. Mike was standing in the open door, beckoning for his friend.

Sam turned to Carole. "I'll go talk with Mike, while you all look around." He looked at the girls. "I'll catch up with you ladies later, okay?"

He turned to Carole, "Save me a seat, if I don't get back to you before show time."

Jessica warned, "You better get back."

"Where're you going?" Savannah asked.

"I'm going over there, to talk with Mike." Sam pointed toward the Clubhouse.

"Go on." Carole waved him away. "Don't pay any attention to them. We'll save you a seat."

Sam looked at the sky. It was already dusk. Not quite dark, but the sun was dropping fast. He knew it would be light for about another hour at the most. Darkness would come quickly.

As he walked toward the Clubhouse, Sam canvassed the revelries. Savannah had certainly described the carnival-like festivities accurately. The exuberant atmosphere intrigued him. He observed the activities with meticulous curiosity.

Mike watched Sam as he crossed the pseudo-midway. He brandished a resilient smile. It was very contagious, and Sam smiled back.

"So," Mike quizzed, "what do you think?"

Sam pressed his lower lip against the upper and shrugged his shoulders. "Like a big carnival, as it was described to me."

"Don't give me that!" Mike snarled stubbornly. "I saw your reaction. You're downright impressed."

Sam tightened his lips. "I must admit that I am amazed to see such an elaborate production like this in Beckham County."

"There. I knew you were impressed."

"Dumbfounded is more like it."

"Me too. I think this has to be the most sophisticated set-up we've ever had for any sort of celebration in this county."

Sam looked back, "What's with all the security?"

"You know what it's for. They're expecting the big bad demon tonight." Mike held his arms out and wiggled his fingers furiously, to imitate a spooky, monster-type effect. He laughed.

"With all the police in the state here? It seems to me the evil spirit could strike any other place in the state tonight without the slightest bit of interference."

Mike snickered. "That's for damn sure. But none-the-less, Jasper says that all the scientific data points to this place and time. The sheriff doesn't necessarily agree completely, but he says the culprit is definitely overdue."

Curious. "Exactly what does he mean? What scientific data points to this place and time?"

"What has come to be called the Monster's MO by the local constabulary is the pattern established over the past ten years."

"A pattern that points to the fireworks display?"

"According to Jasper. . . and Jerome."

Sam looked around. This bit of news impressed him much more than all the festivities.

"Since all the madness about the bones at Clear Creek first emerged," Mike continued, "the people of Culver City have been very precarious. The Mayor and town council were even able to convince the governor to send reinforcements to assist the sheriff for this event."

"Wow. They must be confident the demon will strike."

"Yes. They feel like the evil spirit could take out all these police as easily as if they were a group of sorority girls, but the sheriff and mayor hope he, it, or whatever, will not act with this overwhelming presence of law enforcement."

"So, what do you think?"

"Well, even though the demon could likely subdue the entire contingent of peace officers, as Jasper expects, past history makes me believe he wants to be more discreet about his activities." He looked at Sam, "So does the Sheriff."

"More discreet? The whole damn world seems to know his every activity. Nothing discreet about that."

"No. Just think about it. Nobody actually knows anything. They only have a bunch of wild theories and total speculation. That mass grave over on Clear Creek was discovered quite by accident. Whatever put those bodies there has been doing so a long time . . . for many years."

Sam shrugged.

"There is actually no real proof of anything, so I don't think the evil spirit is ready to show his hand."

"You really think he gives a shit?"

"By all indications, he is one very clever demon. And, for whatever reason, I feel confident he doesn't intend to expose himself at this time."

"It would sure be a shame to disappoint ole Jasper." Sam laughed.

"Yeah," Mike admitted, "it's probably the first time anyone has ever taken that dimwit seriously, but I honestly don't think it will happen . . . at least not here."

"I hope you're right," Sam conceded. "Seems to me we've had enough of this monster crap, with demons and all these unnecessary killings."

"I didn't say he would stop killing," Mike avowed.

"Oh? Do you think he might go elsewhere, or simply lie low for a while?"

"No. I honestly don't believe he can do either."

"Why not?"

Mike stared Sam straight in the eye. "To answer the first question, for some reason, he's tied to this area, with a strong attachment. And for the second, I agree with the sheriff that he takes life in order to survive. He might even take life tonight, and even in this area, but I don't think it will be done openly."

A loud commotion erupted at the far end of the midway. Sam looked toward the noise. Mike stepped from the doorway to get a better view.

People were scrambling. Hordes were scattering from the scene, others were running toward the site. There was mass confusion throughout the midway.

Sam and Mike looked just in time to catch the final seconds of a brilliant light. An intense blue-white flare. They looked at each other, then darted toward the point of havoc.

As they passed through the midway, they saw several bodies strewn about. Paramedics were on the scene instantly. A quick check indicated all the victims were alive, and that four or five needed to be sent to the hospital.

"Wow!" Mike exclaimed. "That sure made my heart flutter."

"Mine, too."

"Did you see that bright light?"

"I sure did. I don't think I have ever seen anything quite like that before."

"For an instant there I thought it was the demon . . . the supernatural spirit, sucking out life."

"You thought it was the demon?"

"Yeah."

"And you ran down here like that?"

"Yeah. What did you think it was?"

"I don't know. I reacted instinctively. I didn't think at all, I just followed you."

Jasper cautiously approached Mike. "The bright light came from a transformer over there." He pointed to a pole nearby. "It exploded, and took out half the lights."

They looked up. In all the excitement, neither Mike nor Sam had noticed how dark it was.

At that moment, Mike saw a dark silhouette streak across the midway in the distant background. Mike looked at Sam to see if he noticed. Apparently, he was talking to Jasper.

Mike turned back around, just in time to see another dark silhouette duck behind a group of spectators.

He looked back at Sam and Jasper.

"Did you see that?" Mike exclaimed emphatically.

Sam and Jasper stared at him.

"See what?" Sam asked. "Be more specific. Exactly what are you referring to?"

Mike was despondent.

"Jasper was telling me something very interesting," Sam added. He turned to Jasper. "Repeat what you just said, I don't think Mike was listening."

"I said we don't know what happened before the explosion," Jasper admitted. "The screams and panic all came prior to the big explosion. No one has any clue as to the reason."

"You mean, there were actually screams and panic before the transformer blew?"

"Several people screamed. People were running in every direction. We were already headed down here when that big transformer erupted so violently. It was indeed a blinding light, but it didn't cause these people any harm. We don't know how they were injured."

The dissertation was suddenly interrupted by a blood curdling scream from the bleachers in the old cemetery. They all three looked and made haste to the scene of this newest occurrence across the road.

It was in a very dark, back corner of the bleacher seats. A few people were huddled around a young woman, who was unquestionably shaken.

When Jasper and Mike reached the scene, Sam and Sheriff McNeal were talking with the distressed young female. Mike looked back in disbelief. He thought Sam was behind him.

The girl was terrified. She suddenly went numb, and quit talking altogether. She couldn't speak.

Sheriff McNeal looked around. He asked if anyone else had seen what happened.

A young girl stepped forward. Jocelyn, a nineteen-year-old, average looking friend of the shaken girl.

"I did, Sheriff. I saw it."

He looked at the young girl. "Good. Can you tell me exactly what happened? As accurately as possible."

Jocelyn hesitated. She took a deep breath to regain her composure. "Sandy was seated there," she pointed, "on the end of the bench. I was on the other side of her." She pointed again. "Right over there."

Everyone looked to see where Jocelyn pointed.

"We were just sitting there talking while waiting for the fireworks show. Sandy made some comment about how spooky it was here since the lights went out on the midway."

She looked up. "I said I thought maybe the lights had gone out here as well."

Everyone looked at the lights.

"We were looking at the lights. Sandy turned, to check the lights behind us." She pointed, "On that post back there."

The sheriff was apprehensive. "Yes?"

"Before I could even look, Sandy screamed bloody murder. It was her scream that scared us."

"Why did she scream?"

An image flashed through Jocelyn's mind. The image of an ambiguous figure in a trench coat, a black trench coat. It changed from a man to a serpent and back again.

"What did you see?"

"There was a man. I saw the same weird looking man that caused Sandy to scream. It was a shadowy figure of a man, standing by that light pole."

"Can you describe him?"

She pointed at Sam. "Like him!"

Everyone looked at Sam.

The sheriff turned back. "Like him?" He pointed at Sam.

The image in her mind was still flashing. The face was changing rapidly. From image to image to image.

Jocelyn studied Sam for a minute, then changed her mind. "No, wait, Sheriff. It wasn't at all like him." She shook her head vigorously and cupped her hands over her face.

"Take your time. Think. Concentrate."

"It didn't look like him, but was the same general shape, maybe the same size . . . I - I can't remember."

Jocelyn was very pale. She was ready to faint.

Mayor Bulan joined the group.

The sheriff quickly attempted to divert the focus. "It's okay. Think about it carefully. Close your eyes and try to focus on his face. Just the face."

Jocelyn gazed into the sheriff's eyes. "I looked right at him. I would have sworn that I could identify him if I ever saw him again. Now, I'm not sure at all. When I try to remember his features, different images keep flashing through my mind. I'm completely befuddled."

"Befuddled? In what way are you befuddled?"

"As soon as I see an image I think is the man I saw, another pops into my head, then I'm positive that's him, then another. I simply can't explain it."

"I can."

Everyone immediately turned toward the voice. Rose, an attractive twenty-two-year-old brunette stepped up.

"You saw him?" The sheriff asked.

"Very clearly."

"Now we're getting somewhere," Mayor Bulan injected with a big smile. "Can you describe him?"

Sheriff McNeal bounced an indignant glare at the mayor. He couldn't determine precisely who was more aggravating, Deputy Jasper, or Mayor Bulan.

"When that girl screamed, I was standing right beside the bleachers. I turned," Rose drew in a deep breath, "and I was staring right into his face." She paused. "And I'm not sure it was a man at all."

"You saw him clearly. You said you can explain this girl's predicament," Jasper mocked, "but you don't even know if it was a man or woman?"

Rose turned defiantly to Jasper. "It was definitely male," she stipulated. "I'm just not certain it was human."

"Not human? Wait just a minute!" Jasper exclaimed. "Are you completely nuts?"

The sheriff laid the palm of his hand across Jasper's chest. "Jasper, let me do the questioning."

Everyone looked at the girl.

"It did appear to be a man standing there," she pointed, "directly under the light."

"Under the light?" The sheriff quizzed. "I thought the lights were out."

"Yeah, the light was not actually burning."

"Oh? Then you mean he was standing in the dark, beside that light pole, back there." He pointed.

"No. He was in the light. I'm not sure how, or what made the light, because that light up there on the pole," she pointed, "was definitely not burning."

"That's just plain crazy," Jasper offered.

"Anyway," she totally ignored Jasper, "as I looked at him, the face gave off a ghoulish glow."

"A ghoulish glow?"

"Yes. He was literally glowing in the dark, and he looked like different men."

"Like different men?" The mayor jumped in again.

"You know, like one, then another, then another, and so on. The face kept changing, very rapidly. That lady over there screamed." She pointed. "That distracted me for a moment. When I looked back, he was gone."

"If you were standing here," Sheriff McNeal calmly noted, "and the man, or whatever, was there. How did he go anywhere else without going past you?"

"He was there," she pointed to the pole. She turned and pointed to the front corner of the bleachers. "Then he was over there. I didn't see him go from there to there, and I looked back to the place he had been, then to the place he was, but he wasn't there either."

She pointed to the top row. "He was up there. I looked at him and he just disappeared altogether."

"Whoa. Slow down. Think about this clearly, and then try to explain to me exactly what you saw."

"I just did, Sheriff. I told you exactly what I saw. He didn't move physically by walking or running, he just sort of flashed from one point to another like a magician, and then vanished completely, before my very eyes."

"She's telling the truth," another man chimed in. Ralph was twenty-eight, handsome, slender and casually dressed.

The sheriff looked at Ralph. "Telling the truth about what, her description?"

"That's right. Her description is pretty accurate. He flashed from one point to another, like a magician. But I would use the word phantom instead of a ghoul."

"Phantom?" The sheriff shook his head. He looked at the woman, who was being checked by the paramedics. He looked around. There had been two very unusual disturbances, yet most of the people were oblivious to the extraordinary activities. They were now filing into the bleachers for the fireworks show.

"One other thing, Sheriff."

"Yes?" He turned back. "What's that?"

"Each time the phantom moved from one place to another, there was a flash of light."

"Flash of light? Bright light? Glowing light?"

"No. A little flash of light. A poof!"

The mayor stepped up next to the sheriff, and quietly whispered into his ear. "Perhaps you can get names and pursue this matter later."

The sheriff looked around to see the bleachers filling with people. Sarcastically, "You want to get on with the show."

"See any reason not to?"

"No. I suppose you're right," he agreed. "We're obviously not getting anywhere with these people tonight."

McNeal conferred privately with his deputies, then turned to announce, "Thank you, for all your information, folks. Jasper will want the name of every person who was here at the time of the incident. We'll want to talk with each of you individually, at a later time."

The sheriff turned to leave.

Jasper got out his pad and pen.

Mike looked for Sam. He was gone again.

Mike spotted him on the opposite side of the bleachers. He was staring into the darkness of the old cemetery. He seemed to be looking toward the corner where his family was buried.

Mike watched Sam for a moment. He wondered when Sam had slipped away. He pondered briefly, looked at the crowd coming into the bleachers, glanced at the starless night and headed for the Clubhouse.

Sam gazed into the shadows of the old graveyard. He studied the obscure silhouettes of decrepit old headstones. He was curious about where his family was buried and somewhat disappointed that he had not pursued the details before now.

Wham! Without warning, Jessica slammed into Sam and wrapped both her arms around his waist. Savannah grabbed his leg and latched on for dear life.

Both girls laughed heartily.

"Hey, Sam. Where ya been?" Savannah yelled.

Carole stretched forward and took Savannah firmly by the shoulder. "Take it easy. You girls let go of Sam."

The girls released Sam and looked up. Savannah took one hand. Jessica took the other.

"Come on, Sam, let's sit over here," Savannah requested.

Sam peered at the terrifying blackness of the old cemetery. The girls tugged eagerly. They were obviously unaware of the unusual activities Sam had just encountered.

"Come on . . . Sam!"

They took their seats. The girls chattered. All Sam heard was a mild roar of indistinguishable tones. He looked at the midway. It was still, deserted. All the people had settled in for the fireworks display.

"How soon forgotten," Sam thought. He considered the possibilities of what might actually be revealed tomorrow. About the alarming events of this frightful night. Everything had drifted back to normal, but the air was heavy with an uncanny aura.

Sam looked around the crowd. He scrutinized the faces one at a time. It was an eerie reminder of the curious onlookers at the Clear Creek phenomena. The same weird cogitations kept running through his mind, *"these people are always there, they are always watching, but never seeing."*

Savannah tugged at his arm.

"Sam! Sam! I'm talking to you."

"Sorry, Savannah. What did you say?"

"They're starting the fireworks."

"It's about time."

"I love fireworks, don't you?"

"I sure do. I like the rockets best. The ones with multiple star-bursts in different colors."

"Me too." Jessica twisted on her bench. She was anxious for the show.

"I like the really loud ones," Savannah added.

It was an exceptionally spectacular exhibition.

Sam looked at his watch when Mayor Bulan finally wished everyone a good night. It was eleven-thirty, quickly approaching the bewitching hour.

The long dark walk from the golf course to their house could be an aghast adventure. There were no stars, no moon. The night was pitch black.

Spectators slowly began to disperse. Sam watched intently as the people went on their way. He looked at Savannah and Jessica and sighed.

"We better head for home," Carole announced.

They stood, stepped over the bench and made their way toward the road.

"I'm sure glad you're with us, Sam," Carole said. "This has been one strange evening, and it's a scary trek to the house on this dark, isolated road."

"Yes," Sam replied. "I'm glad, as well."

Carole's expression suddenly went flat. "Are you sure you're okay, Sam? You look very pale . . . almost ghostly."

Savannah and Jessica both leaned forward to look at him. They showed great concern as well.

"I'm all right," Sam insisted. "It's been a strenuous day. An exasperating evening. I'm tired, that's all."

"Mike will probably give us a ride."

"No. The walk will do me good. The fresh night air is just what I need." He looked into the dark, starless sky and took in a deep breath.

"Are you sure?" She tenderly gripped his shoulder.

"I'm sure." Sam glanced toward the old cemetery.

Sam peered at the departing spectators, then checked his wrist watch once again.

It was nearly midnight. Sam was apprehensive. His total being was wrapped in some strange feeling of finality. Time had run out, and this frenzied sensation was unnerving.

He stopped at Carole's driveway.

"We'll walk you home," she admonished.

"No need. It's not necessary for you to walk me down the hill and then come back up here alone."

"We don't mind."

"Don't be silly. I'll be fine." He looked at Savannah and Jessica. A warm glow flushed through his body. It was difficult for Sam to understand these feelings.

He wasn't certain what was happening to him, but he felt a desperate urgency to get home. He knew he had to be alone. He excused himself very adamantly and trudged down the dark road toward his cabin.

Carole, Savannah, and Jessica reluctantly watched Sam walk away. They were sad. It was a weird feeling they could not explain, but they really did not want to let him go.

He topped the hill without looking back. When he was out of sight, Carole and the girls slowly walked to their house.

They looked into the vast darkness. There was a peculiar mood to the night. The atmosphere was heavy with an eerie supernatural obscurity.

The girls scurried into the house. Carole stared into the sky. She peered pensively toward Sam's house. She simply didn't understand her misgivings.

Finally, she took one last deep breath of fresh night air, and slowly went inside.

Chapter 13

Savannah was playfully chasing Jessica around the front yard when the clamoring ruckus of speeding cars caught their full attention.

The girls stopped abruptly and watched, as four police vehicles zoomed past their house. Sam Pent's house was the only thing beyond this point, and the vehicles made a frightful commotion when they hit the gravel, past the paved road.

No sirens. No flashing lights. Jessica stared at the spectacle in amazement. She suddenly realized there was something dreadfully wrong.

"Mommy! Mommy! They're going to Sam's house!" she screamed as she darted across the yard.

Carole came to the door quickly. "Wait. Jessica, wait! Don't go down there," her voice trailed off to nothingness. Jessica was out of range, and Savannah was close on her heels. Carole was not far behind.

The cars were fanned out around the front and one side of the house. There was one man stationed beside each vehicle. Carole surmised deputies had also gone to the other side of the house, as well as the back.

On closer scrutiny, she detected men were actually hiding beside the cars, with weapons drawn.

Jessica and Savannah stopped at the edge of the road. The girls were holding hands, and they viewed the curious activities unnoticed. However, Carole's arrival immediately caught the sheriff's attention. He held up his hand to stop them.

"You folks stay back. This is a crime scene."

"Crime scene?" Carole screeched. "What sort of crime scene? What's going on?" She was frantic.

Just at that moment, two more cars came speeding to the scene. Carole and the girls barely jumped out of the way and approached the sheriff as the men got out of their vehicles.

One man flashed a badge. "James Hogue, Special Agent, FBI." He extended his hand toward the man with him. "This is Special Agent James Downey."

James Hogue was forty-three, a typical government agent. His partner, James Downey was nearing fifty, and also the typical business suit FBI agent.

The driver of the other car stepped forward and greeted the sheriff. "Hello, Sheriff." He flashed his badge. "Sergeant Dale Ross." He gestured, "This is Detective Charles Flaherty. We're with the State Police; on assignment to the governor's special task force on violent crimes. Our specialty is serial killers."

Dale Ross, forty-four, and his younger partner, Charles Flaherty, around thirty-ish, were not nearly as polished and dignified as the former two officers. They were more typically clean-cut, but more local.

"FBI, state police, sheriff's deputies, serial killers? What the heck is going on here?" Carole demanded.

Sheriff McNeal looked Carole in the eye. "I told you folks to go on home. It's dangerous here."

"We ARE home." She turned and pointed directly at her house. Her voice had definitely jumped a pitch, and she was quickly becoming very angry. "We live right there. Just the three of us. If it's dangerous, we should know why. You tell us right now what's going on."

"Where's Sam?" Jessica tugged at Carole. She looked all around. "What's happened to him?"

"Yeah." Savannah chimed. "Where is Sam, anyway?"

"Can't tell you anything right now," the sheriff admonished.

Another car slowly eased down the road. It stopped, then backed up slightly. Jeri Jacks prudently exited the vehicle. Everyone turned to watch. She carefully closed the car door and headed straight for the sheriff.

Detective Ross took hold of the sheriff's arm. "Who is that woman, Sheriff?"

"It's that nasty old newspaper woman," Jessica blurted indignantly.

"Newspaper woman?" Agent Flaherty replied.

"It's okay," the sheriff asserted, "I invited her."

Everyone looked curiously at McNeal.

"Invited her?" Ross snapped. "You think this is a party?"

"Well, Detective," McNeal's said harshly, "if it is, it's still my party." His dander was definitely aroused.

Jeri could see the antagonistic interaction but didn't hear the precise conversation. She approached, but she suspected her presence was most likely the reason for the austere tone of the dialogue between the Sheriff and the detectives.

She looked meekly at the sheriff, waiting, not really wanting to interrupt the parley. "Thanks for keeping your promise. Am I out of the way here?"

Sheriff McNeal forced a smile. "You're fine, Jeri. Glad you could make it."

All attention turned back to the house. The eerie sensation of anticipation was overwhelming.

"We really do need to know what's going on here," Carole demanded. She glared at Sheriff McNeal.

"Where is Sam?" Jessica insisted.

The sheriff stooped. He looked Jessica in the eye.

"Where do you think he might be?"

"Well, he's not in there," Jessica announced politely.

Everyone looked at her. The sheriff looked at the house. He stood quickly. "Then where might he be?"

Jeri took the sheriff's arm. "What did I tell you?"

"He couldn't have known we were coming." He spoke directly to Jeri, but everyone was keen on their conversation.

"My money's on the brat," Jeri exclaimed confidently. "He's always a step ahead of us."

Jessica threw an angry glare at Jeri. "You better bet on the brat, you nasty old troublemaker."

Jeri flared indignation at Jessica.

The sheriff bent down. "Well, my dear, if Sam Pent is not in that house, we sure are wasting a lot of manpower here."

"Duh-h-h." Jessica's obvious sarcasm nearly made all the spectators laugh, but the situation was far too serious.

McNeal shook his head in frustration.

"How do you know he's not here?" Carole asked Jessica.

She shrugged her shoulders. "I just know."

"Did you see him leave?" Carole questioned.

"No, I didn't see him leave. But I know he's not around here anywhere. I can just tell."

"Yeah, me too," Savannah agreed.

Detective Flaherty looked into the air. "I think she's right, Sheriff. Can't you feel it? He's not here."

"Feel it? Don't be ridiculous!"

"Don't you think he would have come out to see what all this fuss is about?" Carole asked.

"We'll soon find out if he's here or not."

"You still haven't told me what this is all about."

Jasper jumped in, "Sam Pent is a serial killer."

Utter shock. Carole laughed out loud. She looked at the sheriff. "You must be joking. Sam Pent? A serial killer. Now that is what I call ridiculous."

"How about a supernatural demon? Does that fit him any better?" Jasper remarked bitterly.

Carole shook her head. "Just about as likely," Carol replied. She couldn't help but laugh, even though she could tell it was a very serious situation. She muttered to herself, "Serial killer . . . supernatural demon. Hah!"

The sheriff judiciously extended his hand forward and motioned for Jasper to shut up. "Enough!"

Carole looked from Jasper to the sheriff. She didn't know whether to laugh or cry. "Sam Pent. A supernatural serial killer?" She perused the crowd.

"Right now," the sheriff stated, "We just want to talk with him. We need to straighten out a few serious discrepancies."

Carole surveyed the scene. "Talk? You sure have a lot of firepower. Sort of intimidating for a talk, don't you think?"

Savannah tugged at Carole. "Are they going to shoot Sam, Mommy?" she asked.

"They can't," Jessica responded immediately. "I told you, Sam is not even here."

"Good." Savannah was pleased.

McNeal glared at Jessica. "You keep saying that."

The sheriff was unquestionably agitated.

She shrugged. "Because it's true. Go see for yourself."

"That's a good idea, Sheriff," Hogue replied. "Why don't we check it out?"

"Okay." The sheriff scanned his troops. "Watch my back, I'm going in."

Sheriff McNeal approached the front door, with continuous glances back toward his men. The deputies remained alert. The sheriff stood to one side of the door and knocked sharply on the wooden frame.

"Sam Pent, this is Sheriff McNeal," he shouted. "I want to talk to you. Come on out."

Total silence. He waited and listened. Nothing. He looked toward Carole, then knocked again, louder.

"Sam Pent! This is Sheriff McNeal. I want to talk. Come on out, and no one will get hurt."

There was absolute silence.

Jessica tiptoed up to Carole. "I told you Sam wasn't here," she whispered.

Carole bent over. "Where is he, Jess?"

"Gone. He's gone."

"Gone where?"

"I don't know," she shrugged, "just gone. I could always tell when he was home." She looked at Carole. Her eyes began to tear. "Mommy, we'll never see Sam again. I can feel it."

Carole didn't know how to respond. She pulled both girls close. She felt it too, a strange, empty feeling.

Sheriff McNeal cautiously turned the door knob. It was open. He gently pushed the door ajar. The men were ready. He called again, "Pent? You in there?"

Swoosh!

The sound of something flying out the door caused the Sheriff to jump back and instantly raise his gun.

He was flat against the wall. He twirled. Looked in every direction. He didn't see anything. He looked at the door, then quickly back at the deputies. It was obvious they didn't see anything either, but they had all taken cover.

McNeal recovered, and peered inside. "Are you in there Pent?" There was no response. He turned and motioned for the deputies to come in.

Six officers swarmed quickly into the house and dispersed into different areas. Sheriff McNeal followed them inside.

Carole and the others waited patiently.

The sheriff finally came to the front door and signaled all clear. The FBI agents, state troopers, plus Carole, Jeri and the girls slowly entered the house and joined Sheriff McNeal in the living room.

Everything looked normal, as if Sam was just out for an errand, or was somewhere close by.

"No one is here," the sheriff reported.

"I told you," Jessica added sharply.

"He knew we were on to him," Jasper declared. "He must have taken flight."

Jeri raised her eyebrows. "Think about it, he's always been at least one step ahead of us."

Carole frowned at Jeri. "What makes you think Sam's the demon . . . Or a serial killer?"

"Get real, lady."

McNeal looked at Carole. "We've been waiting for some confirmation on several things in our investigation . . . They all came in at once, and they all point to Pent."

"What sort of things?"

"For one thing," the sheriff continued, "Sam Pent is in the group photo taken of the Scout Troop on their outing the day before they disappeared ten years ago."

"You've got a good point, Sheriff. That sure sounds like a serial killer to me." Sarcastically.

"He's the only person in the photo who is not missing."

"Who wasn't missing. He's sure missing now," Jeri replied.

McNeal continued, "We have a witness who says he's the man on the motorcycle."

"The last person to see those two sweet young girls alive in the gorge," Jasper added quickly.

Carole frowned again. "Sam doesn't have a motorcycle."

"The witness identified Sam, not the motorcycle. Anyway, someone else saw him get into the car with those two city slickers from the golf course."

"Wow! This all sounds like a broken fairy tale," Carole said.

"Problem is," the sheriff added, "Pent has never come forth with any of this information. I simply want him to clarify some of the specific details for me. If you want to help clear him, look around. See what's missing."

Carole turned around. "Jess, you know everything in Sam's house, let's look around."

Jessica jerked away. "Help them? Are you crazy?"

"I don't want to help them, Honey. Maybe it will help clear Sam of these ridiculous accusations."

Jessica stared at her mother with serious concern, and she thought about the situation.

They combed every inch of the house.

"Find anything?" the sheriff inquired.

"Just this." Carole handed him a note. "It was on the night stand next to his bed."

"What does it say, Sheriff?" Jasper asked.

Jerome Parks and Mayor Bulan had both come in. Jerome looked over the sheriff's shoulder.

The sheriff frowned and handed him the paper. "What do you make of this, Jerome."

"What's it say, Sheriff?" Jasper asked again.

Jerome looked up. "There are three lines," he remarked.

Jerome read the paper aloud:

"A paradox.

Evil destroys everything.

True love conquers evil."

There was total silence. Everyone concentrated.

141

"Jasper."

"What, Sheriff?"

"Didn't you say Sam Pent had been married?"

"Yeah. He's divorced."

"Does he have any children?"

"Don't know, Sheriff. We could never find any trace of any family whatsoever."

"He has a son," Carole interjected.

Everyone looked at her.

"I never actually met him, but Sam told me he has a son named Richard."

"Richard what?" the sheriff asked.

"Pent." Sarcastic.

"Does he have a middle name?"

"I think it's Evan. Richard Evan Pent."

Jeri shrieked, "Repent!"

Everyone looked at her. Astounded. Curious.

"That's right, Jeri." Sheriff McNeal looked at the FBI agents. "We have to locate his son."

Mayor Bulan looked around the crowd. Confused. "I wish to hell somebody would tell me what's going on."

"He's one step ahead of us, Mayor." The sheriff shook his head. "Always one step ahead."

Jerome approached the sheriff. "Seems like we're through here." He glanced at his watch. "I need to run if you don't need me any more right now."

"Hot date, Jerome?"

Jerome laughed. "Hardly. Our church is going on an outing in the gorge. It's part of the celebration for our one-hundredth anniversary."

"Outing in the gorge? That sounds exciting."

"Yeah, I'm sure." He laughed again. "Actually," he abruptly modified his disposition with a more serious attitude, "it can be fun." His statement was direct and convincing. "We're going to picnic, hike, and some of the kids are going to put canoes into Winding River near Satan's Peak."

The Sheriff was shocked. "Satan's Peak?"

"Yes. In fact," he hesitated, and looked up and down the river, then back toward the sheriff as he continued, "they will make their way all the way down river to the golf course."

"From Satan's Peak to the golf course," Jasper exclaimed. "That's quite a canoe trip."

"Not really. It's downstream all the way. The Boy Scouts used to make that excursion on a regular basis." He looked back at the sheriff. "Is it okay for me to leave now?"

There was no response. Sheriff McNeal had become locked in a trance of sudden realization.

"Golf course," he muttered to himself. *"From Satan's Peak to the golf course. A celebration. The church group, celebrating their one-hundredth anniversary."*

Oblivious to all else, he stood there at the edge of the river, silently staring into the dark water.

Epilogue

Jerome gleefully pushed the twelfth canoe away from the shore, and waved, as the last of the twenty-four adventurers headed downstream.

The one-hundredth anniversary had been quite an exciting event, and this group of young people, which included five adults and nineteen youths ranging in age from fourteen to twenty-six, were ecstatic about their canoe excursion down the wilds of the Winding River, through the scenic gorge.

Approximately ten seconds had been allowed between the launching of each canoe. This precise mathematic calculation would definitely not maintain their pattern for very long.

The celebrants who were left behind, returned to the picnic area to continue their festivities after seeing the last pair off.

Four men were designated to meet the river adventurers at the golf course. They knew the twelve to fifteen mile trip down the river would allow them plenty of time for a few additional refreshments and some general socializing.

The canoes periodically found themselves bunched closely together and bumping, even though their departure had been adequately staggered to prevent this very thing.

The joyful boaters laughed, and splashed, and battled a bit before they would separate to continue on their journey.

It was strictly a fun trip, with no precise schedule to follow, and everyone wanted to make the most of this once in a lifetime adventure on Winding River.

The river was particularly narrow through the gorge, and not very deep in most places. However, it was protected under the "Wild River" program, so every inch was unpredictable.

Besides, these young people had no intention of actually getting into that murky, mysterious water.

The natural scenery was spectacular, and they were now traveling through a deep ravine the river had cut into the gorge over millions of years.

The fantastic cliffs and the magnificent slopes had not been tampered with by man or machine. Pure unadulterated nature, as seen by the very first travelers into this wilderness area hundreds of years ago.

It was the same as viewed by the prehistoric people who roamed this area many thousands of years before the pioneers discovered this gorge. Absolutely awesome.

Something suddenly caused everyone to get ever so quiet, at the same time. They drug their paddles in the water quietly. They looked about and listened attentively. That deafening sound of flashing water, splashing violently against rocks, was getting much louder.

They realized they were fast approaching rapids. No one in this group had been here, and they didn't know what to expect. That's part of what made it so exciting, but now every member of the group was definitely experiencing an adrenaline rush.

Circumstances now demanded that they separate, and form a single-file line through this next portion of their trip.

The lead canoe pulled close to the shore and grabbed a low-hanging branch to hold them stable. They motioned for the others to fall in behind, and when there were five other canoes stopped, the leader in the first one pointed to a distinct landmark boulder a short distance downstream. He told the others that passing that boulder should be the signal for the next canoe to release and follow.

After approximately a mile of shallow rapids, they could all see that everyone made it through safely. That bit of excitement had created quite enough drama to keep this group of novices bragging for many years.

There were no treacherous waters, but the precise, delicate maneuvering created an extended gap between canoes.

It also created another situation.

While traveling through the curving, twisting stream below the rapids, nearly every canoe was out of sight of the others at some point for at least a few minutes.

Finally came a long stretch, followed by a sharp turn, and then more twists and curves.

Even though they were barely within shouting distance of each other, each pair could see three canoes ahead during that long stretch, before the canoe in front disappeared around the sharp turn in the river.

Immediately after the lead canoe was out of view, around the curve, the three following saw a brilliant flash of light come from the approximate position of the first canoe.

The others all looked at each other in dismay but were not close enough together for discussion. They were anxious to get around the curve and see what had caused the aberration.

When the second canoe rounded the bend, just out of sight, the three canoes immediately behind saw another brilliant explosion-like flash of light. They were anxious, concerned, and somewhat scared, but felt their only option was to continue.

When the same thing happened after the third canoe had passed from sight, the pair in the fourth canoe were surely frightened, but those following them were just now experiencing the phenomena freshly.

The men waiting at the golf course had been having an enjoyable visit, not at all concerned that their young adventurers were falling very much behind schedule.

No one really knew exactly how long the trip should take, but some of the more experienced persons in the group had made some intelligent time projections.

Since there were some very experienced outdoorsmen in the group, there was still no reason for any serious concern.

It was not until Jerome accidentally discovered an empty canoe on the shore below the golf course, that a real alarm was generated. That started everyone figuring and guessing.

He was casually exploring the river's edge along the golf course, when he inadvertently came upon the canoe stuck in some trees growing half in the water and half on shore.

Jerome immediately rushed to the other waiting pickups, and together they pulled the craft completely onto the shore for a better inspection.

They soon determined the abandoned canoe was indeed one that had been launched by the church group from Satan's Peak a short while earlier.

He remembered the sheriff had extra forces, who were in town to assist with the Sam Pent situation, and decided to call them for help.

Teams were immediately formed and a thorough search was initiated in both directions from that point where Jerome had found the abandoned canoe.

The firsthand search along the shoreline of the golf course eventually turned up twelve deserted canoes. No people, no signs of struggle, no blood, and not one single indication of any sort of violence.

Just twelve empty boats - abandoned canoes.

The citizens of Beckham County were once again thrown into a turmoil of mass hysteria.

An extensive three-day search, both up and down the river, turned up absolutely no signs of the missing persons, and not one solitary clue as to what might possibly have happened.

Sheriff McNeal sat mutely at his desk. He was thoroughly perplexed. The haunting words of Jasper kept running through his boggled mind. *"The next catastrophic tragedy will take place about here, in early July."*

The sheriff looked at the map. He could still see Jasper's finger pointing to the area of the golf course.

www.ingramcontent.com/pod-product-compliance
Lightning Source LLC
Chambersburg PA
CBHW060123260626
47160CB00005B/2002